SCENT
of
ROSES

PEGGY LOCKWOOD

SCENT OF ROSES
Copyright © 2021 by Peggy Lockwood

All rights reserved. No part of this publication may be reproduced, distributed, or transmitted in any form or by any means, including photocopying, recording, or other electronic or mechanical methods, without the prior written permission of the publisher or author, except in the case of brief quotations embodied in critical reviews and certain other noncommercial uses permitted by copyright law.

Although every precaution has been taken to verify the accuracy of the information contained herein, the author and publisher assume no responsibility for any errors or omissions. No liability is assumed for damages that may result from the use of information contained within.

Library of Congress Control Number: 2021914944
ISBN-13:   Paperback: 978-1-64749-569-5
           Epub: 978-1-64749-570-1

GoToPublish LLC
1-888-337-1724
www.gotopublish.com
info@gotopublish.com

CONTENTS

PROLOGUE 1
CHAPTER 1 4
CHAPTER 2 8
CHAPTER 3 10
CHAPTER 4 13
CHAPTER 5 16
CHAPTER 6 19
CHAPTER 7 21
CHAPTER 8 24
CHAPTER 9 28
CHAPTER 10 32
CHAPTER 11 35
CHAPTER 12 41
CHAPTER 13 43
CHAPTER 14 44
CHAPTER 15 48
CHAPTER 16 50
CHAPTER 17 54
CHAPTER 18 56
CHAPTER 19 60
CHAPTER 20 63
CHAPTER 21 65
CHAPTER 22 67
CHAPTER 23 68

CHAPTER 24	71
CHAPTER 25	74
CHAPTER 26	76
CHAPTER 27	81
CHAPTER 28	83
CHAPTER 29	86
CHAPTER 30	90
CHAPTER 31	93
CHAPTER 32	95
CHAPTER 33	97
CHAPTER 34	99
CHAPTER 35	102
EPILOGUE	104

PROLOGUE
Year 1838

There was nothing soft about the wind. It had almost an eerie sound as it wound its way through the trees. It was a good accent for the haze over the nearby hills. With it came a sound like a million horses' hooves pounding the hard earth as they raced for the finish and the prized blue ribbon.

Bridgitt could hear the sound from her kitchen, where she stood at the sink peeling potatoes for the evening meal. She hated this time of night when she was alone in the house waiting for Jim to come in out of the woods. Jim worked for a lumber mill and spent all day cutting trees for his company. When they first moved to the village, she thought how peaceful and beautiful everything was. Jim had been offered the job just weeks after they were married and it was like a wedding present from above. A new life together.

It was a bright summer morning the day they arrived, blossoms on the trees with gold streaks shining through. Following directions on the sheet they had been given; they drove to the mill office. The owner and Jim's new boss, Mr. Bradshaw, took them on a tour and introduced them to the other employees. Everyone was very friendly and welcomed them to what they called the family.

After a quick tour of the mill, Mr. Bradshaw drove them a short distance into the country and their new home.

There was a lane lined on both sides with poplar trees. The sun did not break through the trees as it had back in the village, and it was almost too quiet. Bridgitt had always lived in a village so she decided that this was just the way of the country. Then she had her first glimpse of the house and lost her heart forever. The stately stone two-story building sat back in a grove of trees that put the border trees to shame. Green velvet grass hugged flower beds bursting with reds and yellows. A red stone walkway wound its way up the steps to a large cedar door beckoning them into a deep cool interior.

As she stood at the kitchen sink, she wondered if even back then there were signs, and she refused to see them for the beauty of the place. The sound was louder now as phantom horses pushed their way to the finish line. Bridgitt lifted the corner of the white lace curtains and peered out into the darkness. Leaning forward, she could see over the hill that led to the village. There just over the hill the light was bright as mid-day and the noise seemed to pound in her ears. She could see lights wavering as if blown by a giant wind. Suddenly, she realized the lights were torches held by a great crowd of people coming towards her house. Their bodies were outlined by the redness in the sky caused by the torches held high before them. Sudden fear filled her, and she pulled away from the window as the fire of the night filled her house. Suddenly, frightened, she wondered where Jim was.

She was here alone with no one to help her. She felt the danger all around her with nothing to protect her against it. The noise became deafening, and the sky was so bright with heat she could almost feel it on her skin. She ran from the kitchen to the stairs in the hall making her way up the steps. She would wait here until they were gone. If she were very quiet, they would think she wasn't home and leave. The sound of feet on the path told her they were almost at her door. Where could she go if they broke the door down and came into the house? They would know to look upstairs if they came in. Her fear was all that kept her from crying out. She pushed her body tight against the wall, feeling the rough roses in the wallpaper scratching against her skin. When Jim wanted her to change the paper, she said no she wanted to feel like she was always in a beautiful garden even when she was in the house. Now, she felt comfort leaning against it.

The sound of the front door crashing in brought her back to reality. She was aware of many pounding feet coming towards her. She turned her head into the flowers. They felt almost real now, soft and fragrant as the ones on her doorstep. As the door burst open, Bridgitt closed her eyes, leaned into the scent, and was gone. From the bottom of the stairs, several men shone their lights. There was no one there. The crowd searched the house in vain, finally turned away, and closed the door on emptiness.

CHAPTER 1
Year 2000

Rain pelted the windshield faster than the wiper blades could handle. It was hard enough driving on unfamiliar roads, but with the rain, it was almost impossible. The trip had come as a surprise as had the house. Karen had made an offer on an apartment closer to her office and thought that finally her life was about to return to normal. Nothing had been normal since her Dad died and until now, she thought nothing would. Her mother died two years before, and she thought she knew her father well. But at his death, she found there were things she had yet to learn for now she was told about the house. Karen thought everything had been settled at her father's death. He had been ill for two years, and she had moved home to care for him. They had become very close and had spent many days reminiscing about the past so, when at his death the house issue came, she was more than a little surprised.

Many hours with Mr. Miller, the family lawyer, were spent tying up loose ends. In the process of sorting all the legal papers, Mr. Miller had found the deed to a house just outside Boston. It had belonged to her paternal grandparents and had not been lived in since her grandfather died. Her parents had never mentioned a house or had there been much said about her grandparents. Now it seemed before it could be sold, she would have to assess the condition for herself before the real estate company would list it. It was for this reason that after closing her office for the weekend, she was now driving into dusk to the old family estate.

The sun had started to set before she was out of the city, and Karen realized now she should have left earlier. Not having allowed for the weekend traffic or the weather, she would be arriving after dark. She had also taken too much time choosing what to take with her. Wardrobe had never been a problem as most of her weekends were spent in jeans and sweats, but since these people didn't know her, she packed a few business outfits. She loved to run and every Saturday at daybreak she set out, her long brown ponytail flashing behind her, for the Bagel Spot to pick up her coffee before heading to the park. She had become a regular to the point that if she didn't show, the store manager would check to see if she was alright, when she took a morning off. So, she dropped around to let them know she wouldn't be there for at least two weeks, so they wouldn't worry. Checking her mirror, she tucked a wisp of hair back from her forehead giving a critical look at her face. Her father had always said her lucid brown eyes reminded him of a little puppy she had as a child, who had a look that no one could resist. She smiled at the thought. With one final look, she turned away.

Picking up her cell phone, she dialed the number her lawyer had given her for the Real Estate office that was looking after things until she arrived. At least she could check and see if there would be hydro. She did not fancy having to cope with candles the first night. After six rings, she was reasonably assured that this office had also closed for the weekend to travel wherever they traveled at the close of the week. She would just have to cope when she got there.

The drive hadn't been an unpleasant one. The sun had set rapidly so she had missed the final color as it slipped over the water's edge. The city lights had been left behind and there had been a feeling of peace settling over everything around her. Different from her day to day life in the city, she thought, as even her weekends had a certain rush to them. Life was fast moving with her private life as well as her job. Not that she was that social but rather just an inner fast pace that kept up with the city noise and glitter. These next two weeks in a small village were sure to prove different.

The last few miles, the rain that had started as a light one had become heavy and made visibility poor. She had pushed on at a slower speed than was normal because of this. Leaning forward, she peered through the pelting rain for a better view. She suddenly realized she had reached the road on the map that would lead her to the house and turned carefully off the main highway onto a dirt road. There were no lights ahead, but according to the instructions, she had been given the house was about five miles up this road. Her 1990 Volkswagen had not been built for these roads, for the ruts that had obviously been there before the storm were now filling up with water making it difficult to maneuver. She had the Volkswagen checked over before she left Boston, but it was an old pampered car used to good solid roads beneath it.

Deciding she must have taken a wrong turn as she was sure she had gone the suggested five miles, she stopped in the middle of the road to decide her next move. She knew there was no turning back as it had been hard enough getting this far. However, if she didn't see a house in the next five minutes she was going to try just that. Starting the car again, she managed to make it over the next knoll and suddenly there it was, the house. It didn't look welcoming. Although the only light she had were the headlights of the car, one look said the house had been neglected for many years. The pelting rain gave it a sinister look, and Karen had a feeling that coming here alone had been a bad idea. Several of her friends had offered to come with her but two weeks on her own had seemed like a wonderful idea. Now she wished she had thought things out more, and there was a friendly face at her side.

Stepping out of her car, she realized suddenly the rain had stopped, and the moon came from behind the clouds giving her full view of what she had inherited. Four large pillars supported what appeared to be a shelter over the front door. Stone steps led to a vast door with windows on both sides. She stood for a long moment trying to decide whether to go in or make her way back to the village until morning. The house would surely look less foreboding in daylight. She reached into her pocket and felt for the key to the house. Foolish she thought, there was no way she was going to struggle back down that muddy road after finally making it this far. After just a moment's hesitation, she closed the car door and turned the lock. Well here goes she thought and headed for the front door, key in hand.

CHAPTER 2

Dan had always been fascinated by the Simpson house. Each day as a child, he had pedalled his bike up the road and stopped at the gate. Some of the kids had told him it was haunted, and he always hoped he would see at least one ghost when he rode by, but alas none had appeared. Now as a man, the house still held him and he stopped at least once a week just to look. Tonight, the board meeting had been a long one so it was late when he passed the house. He intended to give it just a casual look and then head home. However, as he rounded the corner and slowed at the gate, he was surprised to see lights in the house. There shouldn't be lights, and although it had been rumored that the new owner would be arriving, they were not expected until the end of the month. The only person other than the realtor with a key was old Joe the caretaker, and he wouldn't be here at this time of night. Poor old Joe, brave as he was in the daylight, would not hazard a visit with a resident ghost.

Pulling into the lane, he took note of a car with a Boston plate which did fit the new owner. They must really want to sell to come up at least two weeks early. He had told the realtor he was interested in buying but it might be wise to call the next morning just in case there were others looking as well.

Turning the car around, he started up the lane for home. Had he looked back as he always did when leaving what he considered his house, he would have seen in the upstairs window a wisp of grey fog surrounding the pane. It lingered for a moment as though watching him leave then faded back into the shadows of the house. He would also have seen the flutter of curtains at the house next door and the eyes watching him from there. His only thought at this moment however, was the possibility that finally his dream had come true and he would be able to buy the house. As his car disappeared from sight, there was only a suggestion that something might be wrong with this house and he should look elsewhere, but after waiting so long, he was not about to pass up the opportunity to own it. He would worry about any problems when the deed was signed and it was his.

CHAPTER 3

Karen had stood at the front door of the house for some time before she finally put the key in the lock. She found her heart racing, and she was unable to turn the key. What is wrong with me, she wondered. With all the years I've lived in Boston I've never been nervous or afraid even with all the crime city people live with daily. Why do I feel this way now about a harmless empty house? Shaking off what she felt was exhaustion from the long drive, she placed her hand on the door frame.

She felt a tingle up her back as the heavy door moved under her hand. Reaching in, she felt for a light switch and breathed a sigh of relief as the hall filled with light. At least the hydro service was prompt. To her surprise, the hall was freshly cleaned with not a cobweb in sight. As she made her way through the rooms, she found them equally as clean, floors freshly cleaned and no dust covers. Not too strange as the Real Estate from were no doubt out for the listing and making a good impression. For the next half hour, Karen wandered through the downstairs trying to get a feel of her parents in the house. It simply didn't fit.

She shuddered to think of her mother in this old-fashioned kitchen. The sink boasted a rusted pump, suggesting this was the only way water was allowed into the house. She ran a finger around the rim of the sink. It too had been recently cleaned. Even the pitcher used for priming sparkled. She lifted the lid on the wood stove and found it freshly laid for a new fire. She dropped the lid back and looked around. Who she wondered would ever buy such an old house? Visions of being stuck with an old relic flashed before her eyes. She felt very tired. The trip was finally beginning to take its toll.

Wandering through the formal dining room and what she supposed was the parlour, she did notice that even though the kitchen had not been updated the rest of the house was more modern and nicely decorated. Her father must have hired someone to update over the years. Her eyes were starting to burn and tiredness was taking over. She would take a better look in the morning, tonight she needed her bed. Turning off the lights, she made her way into the hall where she had dropped her suitcase.

It was now as she made her way up the stairs that she noticed the old wallpaper in the staircase. Unlike the rest of the house, the staircase had not been redecorated. The wallpaper was very old fashioned. Beautiful paper on its day but now very outdated. The deep rose pattern hadn't been produced in years. It was like something she had seen in an old movie. She reached out to touch the brocaded flowers and gold leaves. Suddenly, she pulled back her hand. The wall had been cold to touch. She thought it might be a breeze or a draft, then realized this was foolish as there wasn't a window in the staircase. For a moment, Karen stood holding her breath as the air became warm again. Her imagination was really running wild tonight.

Starting up the stairs once more, she could hardly wait to get to her bedroom with the pink rosebuds and filmy white curtains at the window. Now where did that come from? Glancing once more at the rosebud covered paper, she still felt something holding her there. What nonsense, how could pink rosebuds on a wall hold her? With a laugh she climbed the final steps. Four doors faced her. Three bedrooms and a bathroom she remembered from the floor plan. She found the bathroom, the first on her right and reaching in turned on the taps happy to find there was water in the house. The next would be a bedroom, and she decided no matter what it was like it would be hers. She didn't think she could take another step. She slowly opened the door and burst out laughing.

"Well, I wasn't wrong on this one," she said. There was a large inviting walnut four poster bed with matching dressing table. A granny rocker with cushions that matched the rose coverlet on the bed and over a wide bay window the white filmy curtains moved gently over rosebud wallpaper.

A sudden wisp of cold air filled the room, and Karen pulled her jacket closer around her shoulders. There must be a draft she thought but was unable to make herself go into the room to investigate. She listened for any sound of wind coming through an open window, but there was none. Everything was quiet except for a soft humming sound that must be a motor somewhere in the house. Then as though nothing had happened, the room was warm again. Well, she thought that was a good show of imagination. I really must be tired from the long trip. With a laugh, she entered the room and threw herself across the bed. Her last thought was of making new curtains for the kitchen as she dropped off to sleep to the warm hum around her.

CHAPTER 4

In the house next door, the morning sun fluttered through the white gauze curtains unto Edna Thornton causing tiny magic lights on her silver coiffed hair. It was a magic room, and the early sun seemed to cast a spell that suggested fairies lurking in every corner. Edna believed in fairies and sitting as she was in her favorite chair, she could almost hear them whispering to each other as they went about their morning chores. For a moment, she pulled her eyes away from the window and took stock of her surroundings. It still had all the original furnishings her grandfather used when he was alive. The overstuffed couch faced the fireplace, and the bookshelves took up one entire wall, his books still in place. Nothing changed even to his pipe, and the humidor perched on the mantle. It was a man's room obviously but Edna found solace here more than anywhere else in the cold rambling old house. Yet she wished she could sell it and move closer to the village.

Once more, she turned to the window and gazed out across the small yard at the house next door. No, she couldn't leave. She could never leave as long as that house was still standing. The house Edna thought. It had been empty for so many years and now suddenly had a new owner. She had seen the lights late last night while she was enjoying her evening brandy. Whoever had moved in had taken the rosebud room. She wondered if they knew the history of the house. Well, she thought sitting back, it wasn't up to her to tell them. Possibly the fairies would. She could hear them whispering away to themselves, as if she couldn't hear them.

Taking her binoculars from the shelf under her chair, she gently pulled the curtains aside. There, just at the bedroom window she saw movement. She adjusted the glasses for a better look. It was a young girl, not someone local, but she seemed familiar to Edna. Why was she waving? The very idea she thought, letting the curtains drop, I don't even know her. She slipped the glasses back onto the shelf thinking she would be more careful the next time she used them. Just as she started to leave the room, she noticed someone walking up the pathway to the house. She stepped closer to the window so she could peer through without moving the curtains.

Shelby, well that wasn't a surprise. The house must be for sale, for only a sale would get Shelby out of bed this early in the morning. Edna had to give her niece credit though she had worked her way up to one of the top real estate salespeople in the area. Her picture was all over the papers and stuck up on posters in every empty spot available. Edna smiled to herself. Let's see her sell this one, no one else had been able to. Many had tried but something always stopped interested parties before the papers were signed. It might be fun to watch Shelby meet her match in the house. She stepped back into the room just as Mary brought in her morning tea. Yes, it just might.

Edna had never been very fond of her sisters' child and even less since Eileen died. Shelby had always thought that she should have a share in the family home now that her mother was gone. It didn't matter that the house had been left solely to Edna or that the money she had been left was all that the will allowed her. She still put in the weekly visit to Edna trying to charm her way into more. A lot of good it would do, Edna thought, for Shelby would get nothing more as long as she was alive. As it was Edna was keeping track of all the things that miraculously disappeared each time Shelby visited. She would make sure there was a recounting of this very soon. She dropped the curtain and with a satisfied smile on her face left the room.

CHAPTER 5

It was to be their first dinner party. They had asked a few of Jim's fellow workers and their wives over for the evening, and Bridgitt decided it might be a good time to try out some of the recipes in the book her mother had given her when they were married. She had found a wonderful sounding recipe for pot roast that didn't seem too complicated for her first try. All morning she had been preparing the vegetables and baking pies and was now ready to tackle the table and decorations. She would have to unpack some of their wedding presents as all they had in the cupboard were enough dishes for the two of them day to day. Jim had put everything else in the attic until she was ready to set the house up more permanently. She dusted the four off her hands and setting her apron aside, headed for the attic door.

Bridgitt had hesitated going into the attic as the staircase was dark, and it seemed rather foreboding. She touched the switch at the bottom of the stairs, throwing a dull light upwards into the dark. The steps were heavy with dust marked only by the footsteps Jim had made taking up their boxes. Taking a deep breath, Bridgitt took hold of the rail and slowly made her way up into the deep shadows.

The attic turned out to be much larger than she thought it would be, and Jim had put the boxes on the far wall making it necessary for her to cover the whole room just to find what she wanted. She pulled out the box marked linens to take down and started searching further for crates marked china. As she moved boxes aside, she found an old brown trunk tucked in the far corner. She didn't remember a trunk with their things. Perhaps, it was left behind by the last people living in the house, it might even be empty she thought.

Curiosity getting the best of her, she pulled the trunk closer and reached for the latch. There was a sudden gust of air and the room became very dark as the latch released and Bridgitt found herself gasping for breath. It was like a vice had tightened around her, and she felt herself falling to the floor. Then as suddenly as it started it was over. Bridgitt lay quietly for a moment trying to make some sense out of what had just happened. She realized that the room was just as light as it had been when she came up and that nothing had changed in the attic. I must be over tired from all the work this morning, she thought, picking herself up from the floor.

Looking around, she once again noticed the trunk only now it was open. Yes, she was about to check the old trunk. She peered into the trunk at what she thought looked like a pile of old dishes. Why there might be something she could use for tonight's dinner. She slowly pulled one plate from its wrapping and was delighted at what she had found. One by one she opened the dishes and pulled them from the trunk. Why there was more than enough for what she needed and not a chip or crack in any of them. Holding one of the plates closer to the light, she was surprised to find that the whole set was black. That colour was a wonderful idea for her table setting. She would just slip into town and pick up black table napkins and black candles, and it would make a beautiful setting. She might even find other black accessories that would give the room a formal look. Picking up as much as she could carry, she started down the stairs to prepare for what she hoped would be a successful evening for Jim.

CHAPTER 6

Karen opened her eyes to a room full of rosebuds. It took her a moment to realize where she was and why there were thousands of rosebuds on her wall. That, she thought, would be one of the first things she would attend to. Who could bear to wake every morning to rosebuds? She knew Jim would not be too happy about this kind of decorating. Now where did that thought come from? She didn't even know a Jim, at least not one she remembered and why should he care about what kind of wallpaper she had in her bedroom?

Outside the sun shone, and the birds taking advantage of a good day chirped merrily in the trees. The sounds were so different from back in Boston. The morning sounds she was used to were traffic and the nosey couple in the adjoining apartment. She slipped out of bed and went to the window. Lifting the curtains, she raised the window to the smell of lilacs blooming in the yard. There was the sound of shears clipping, and she realized it was coming from her own yard. Leaning out, she found there was an elderly man carefully working away at the hedge that divided the two houses. That must be Joe, the caretaker, she thought. He was probably responsible for the house being prepared for her when she arrived. She would dress and go down to meet him.

As she pulled back in, her eye caught a flash of light coming from the next house, almost like a reflection on glass. Why it was a reflection on glass, the glass on a pair of binoculars being used by someone on the lower level of the house next door. The curtains were open just enough for Karen to see they were being used by a silver haired elderly woman. Well, at least the part about nosey neighbours hadn't changed. Karen lifted her hand and waved. She had to chuckle at how fast the curtains were closed. If her neighbour thought she was going to see something interesting in Karen's life, she was going to be very disappointed. No one lived a more boring life than she, and at the moment, it didn't look like there were to be many changes.

Her thoughts were interrupted by the ringing of the downstairs bell. Who could be ringing at this early hour. Not a friendly neighbour with a plate of homemade cookies she hoped, knowing that small towns did this sort of thing. It was probably someone for Jim. He had some new friends at work and was in the shed and didn't see them arrive. As she made her way down the stairs, everything suddenly became dark. Almost as if the sun had gone behind a heavy cloud.

When she left her bedroom, the sun had been shining but now out in the hallway even with a window everything seemed dark. The weather certainly changed in a hurry. She had started down the stairs when once again, she thought who was Jim? After hesitating for just a moment with this thought, she continued down. Automatically, she reached for the light switch in the hall and the door knob at the same time. Just as she touched the door knob, the hall was filled with sunlight. The sun must have been just behind a cloud, Karen thought. Putting it from her mind, she took her hand from the switch and opened the door.

CHAPTER 7

Dan pulled into the parking lot of his office building one hour earlier than usual. Last night seemed to go on forever. He couldn't seem to get the house out of his thoughts. It seemed so close to being his. He had finally given up on sleep and dressed. After two cups of coffee and a brisk shower, he headed for the office. Going in early, he could clear up a few things before the village Real Estate office opened. He felt an urgency that he should be there when they opened. He had become almost obsessed with the idea of owning that house. Dan remembered as a child pedaling his bike past the house and longing to be allowed inside. He didn't know why, but he knew that he had to have the house and needed to make an offer today before anyone else had a chance. He had to have this house; the one from his childhood.

Unlocking the door to his office, he met the smell of fresh polished leather. He always knew what day it was by the smell of his office. No calendar was ever needed as every Monday like clockwork Mrs. Sullivan polished and scrubbed until his office gleamed. However, before Monday came around again the polish smell was gone, and it was back to a mixture of everyday office smell. Dan heard the outer door open and soon there was a tap on his door. It looked like someone else left their bed early this morning. Jeff Curtis, his oldest friend popped his head in. They had been school chums and carried on their friendship through college and later into the business world. Single like Dan, Jeff always had a new girl or a new adventure that invariably included Dan.

"You're in early," Jeff said, adjusting the chair at the desk so he could put his feet up.

"Just finishing up from yesterday," Dan replied. "I have to be away from the office and it could mean the whole day. By tonight, I should be the proud owner of the Simpson place."

"Not that house again," Jeff said. "This has been a thing with you since grade school. You know it's haunted and still you are determined to buy it.

There are dozens of houses on the market right now. Why this one?"

"Just fnishing up from yesterday," Dan replied. "It's that I want to buy that house, and I don't believe it's haunted. That was just kid stuff, and you know it. We just told that story to scare the girls."

"It did scare them too didn't it?" Jeff laughed. "They always moved a bit closer when we drove by the house."

"Yes," Dan laughed, "and we sure drove by the house as often as possible."

Still laughing, Jeff left for his own office. Mary Anne Keller thought Jeff, now there was one that scared easy. Funny he hadn't thought of her in years. Wonder where she moved to? May have to look into that. For now, there was Shelby Thorton. Shelby had been a regular since high school, and Jeff knew that she thought one day, their on and off relationship would become a permanent one. Actually, he was beginning to think that way himself until he thought of Mary Anne. Maybe he and Shelby had known each other too long. Maybe it was time to start cutting the strings; after all it wasn't as though they were engaged. They simply dated because they had always dated every weekend since school. Too permanent, he thought as he unlocked his office door.

Dan finished the rest of his files, and leaving them with a note for his Secretary, he left the building. It was still too early for the real estate so he decided to stop in for a second cup of coffee. The coffee shop was busy with most of the tables full. It meant having to sit at the counter, which annoyed him as a rule, but this morning he was going to start everything with a positive attitude. He took the stool nearest the door and waited for Gillian, the morning waitress to finish serving at the other end. He could see one of his old school mates Hank Johnson out of the corner of his eye and hoped he was too busy to notice who sat at the other end of the counter. Not that Hank was a problem, but since becoming a father, all he could talk about was baby's first smile, baby's first tooth and now baby's first word, which of course, was Da Da. What was it about newly married friends and new fathers that they had to make their old single buddies aware of what they were missing? Not for him. The most important thing for him in life was his house.

There would be time for this kind of thing, if at all when he was well established and the proud owner of his house. He finished his coffee and pushed off the stool. By the clock on the wall, the real estate office should just be opening. Time to go and put things into motion.

CHAPTER 8

Karen opened the door to a well-dressed woman in a no nonsense business suit. She was well groomed and did not carry the tell-tale plate of cookies. The young woman extended her hand before Karen had a chance to completely open the door.

"Shelby Thorton" she said. "I'm with Thorton Real Estate in the village. I was about to visit my aunt next door when I saw a car in the drive. Since the house hasn't been lived in for many years, and the new owner isn't expected till the end of the month I thought I should at least take a look. I expect since you are already in the house you must be the new owner."

"Yes, I am, arriving a bit earlier than expected," Karen replied. "There is however more work to be done here than I thought, so I won't be able to list it at present."

"Oh, surely not that much." Shelby said. "It hasn't been lived in for years, but old Joe has made sure the maintenance was kept up. He has a cleaning service come in once a week and he keeps the gardens himself. I'm sure we could have an offer within weeks if you let me list it today."

Karen bristled slightly as Shelby pushed past her and into the hall. "There is also the chance I won't be selling the house," she said. "I've always wanted to live in the country and this may be my chance."

Why on earth, Karen thought, did she say that? She had no intention of keeping the house. Nothing, absolutely nothing would entice her to spend the rest of her days in a village this small. Her whole life had been spent in Boston, and she couldn't imagine living anywhere else.

She had a good job, and at this moment, was looking for an apartment downtown to be more in the swing of things. Never in this remote place. She put it down to this young woman's abrasiveness and nothing more.

"Well now that you're in, would you like a cup of coffee?" she offered coolly. "I was just about to pour one for myself."

"Why I'd love one and maybe take a peek through while I'm here and give you an idea what you should do before you show the house."

She apparently was very thick-skinned Karen mused as she either missed or ignored the tone of Karen's voice. She chatted about handling the listing herself and Karen would not have to come in unless there was an offer that appealed to her. Karen handed Shelby her coffee and sat down at the table to watch this woman at work. I could really use her at the office, she thought, no one would get past her without leaving a pint of blood and a sample of DNA.

"Now before I start my little tour, I should call my office and let them know where I am in case they need me. Being the owner, they do rely on me, you know. No one seems to be able to make a decision when I'm not there."

'No one is given a chance,' thought Karen. "Of course, the phone is there just right of the door," she said.

While Shelby called her office, Karen wandered back into the hall to close the front door. She had been so surprised when Shelby entered the house that she had left it open. Suddenly she stopped. It couldn't be. It must just be my imagination or still not enough sleep after the trip. This is a strange house and a strange village. Also, I may not be fully awake. Still she would swear there were more roses on the wallpaper than there had been last night. She crossed to the staircase for a closer look. "Yes, I'm sure there are more and they're closer together." She reached out a hand to touch them.

Suddenly, she drew back. "Don't touch the wall," a voice said. Karen stopped. Don't touch the wall. Why shouldn't she touch the wall? Nonsense, she thought. Reaching over to touch one of the roses, she suddenly felt something pulling her. She pulled her hand back in terror. Jim, she had to get Jim. She was all alone, and they were coming for her.

"Terrible paper, isn't it." Karen jumped at the sound of a voice. Shelby was standing behind her. "Imagine seeing that many roses every time you opened the door. There must have been a sale when the decorating was done. I understand there are other rooms with the same paper."

"Only one other," Karen said. "One of the bedrooms." She hoped that Shelby did not hear the tremor in her voice. She realized she was shaking and lowered her hand before Shelby noticed. Where had she been? If it hadn't been for Shelby coming in, she might not have been able to get back. Shelby started up the stairs with book and pencil in hand as if nothing had happened. "Shall we get started?" she said. Karen took one final look at the mass of roses beside her, and keeping well to the banister side, she followed Shelby upstairs.

CHAPTER 9

Karen was finally able to close the door on Shelby's back. *There is no way I could spend more than an hour with her*, she thought. She had wanted to go through the house making up a list of the things that needed looking after before she went shopping. It had been her plan to go into the garden to introduce herself to Joe and leave him with a list. She was sure he would know the right people needed to look after things. Now it would be just a short list as she had seen Joe's truck going up the lane when she saw

Shelby out. That list would just have to wait until tomorrow. She had the sinking feeling that she was going to be here longer than two weeks. For now, there were groceries to buy as Jim would be home for supper soon, and there wasn't much in the house to eat.

The grocery store was busy when Karen pulled into the parking lot so it took some time to find a parking space. She wondered if she should come back later but decided that would mean driving back out to the house and starting all over again. Now or never, she thought. Locking the door and dropping the keys into her pocket, she squared her shoulders and started across the lot. She was surprised at the size of the store for such a small town. It seemed to carry everything a person would need. More than she would ever need for her short stay.

Karen wandered up and down the aisles filling her basket. She picked up fresh fruit and vegetables along with a large assortment of canned goods, wondering briefly why she was stocking the cupboards so well when she was staying for just a short period. Still she did need food, and if her stay turned out to be longer than she had anticipated, she would not go hungry. As she passed the pet aisle, she stopped to check the dog food. Karen had never had a pet but she had always thought that if she did it would be a dog. All the cute little pictures on the cans and boxes certainly tempted her.

"Small dog or large one?" a voice said.

"I beg your pardon," Karen replied.

I said, "Do you own a small dog or a large one."

"Oh no, I don't own a dog. I just like to look at all the food. With all the pictures of those cute animals, it's as much a temptation for people to own a dog as it is for the dogs to eat the food."

"You're right about that," he laughed.

Karen was suddenly aware of the body behind the voice. Dark and moderately handsome, he leaned against his shopping cart just behind her. He had soft brown eyes not nearly as intense as her own and a charming smile. Not much taller than Karen, he had a well-tanned body that suggested the love of the outdoors that she had. First contact in the village, she thought, and she had absolutely nothing to talk about but dog food, then only the pictures on the packages. They probably aren't even real dogs, she thought. Now in the produce department she could have at least talked about the price of tomatoes.

"I have a small dog," he said. "Most men are expected to have large menacing ones to suit their personalities."

"And have you a large menacing one," she asked? "Dog I mean." "No," he laughed. "I just prefer the small loving ones. Dogs I mean."

"Oh, by the way," he said, reaching for her hand. "Dan Purcell. Sorry to interrupt your art appreciation tour."

Karen smiled. "I'm Karen Warren. I'm just in town for a short stay while I sell my house."

Dan took a better look at the woman across from him. So, this is the new owner he thought. This may be the inside track I was looking for. Karen watched closely at the change of expression on Dan's face when he realized who she was. Why would this make a difference to him, she wondered.

"I'm just putting in some provisions for the time I will be here. I really should finish as I had rather a late start, so if you will just let go of my hand I have to get on with it."

Dan realized he was still holding her hand since the introduction. "Oh, sorry," he said as he released her hand. "I tend to wander sometimes."

"Quite alright," she smiled, pushing her cart away from him. "It was very nice meeting you."

"Yes, the same here,'" he replied as she disappeared around the corner.

Well that was a good first impression, he thought. I tend to wander sometimes. What kind of statement was that? He reached up and took down a box of dog food with a cute little white terrier on the front. He had started Snuffy on this one because if he hadn't known better, he'd have thought she posed for it. Dropping it in his basket, he continued on to the cash registers at the front. He saw Karen loading her Volkswagen out front.

Not at all the kind of car he imagined her in. First impressions had given him a rather mildly sophisticated well-dressed city business type. She looked far from this in her jeans and tank top with a wayward ponytail bouncing on her shoulders. There was something about her that seemed familiar. He decided that he would learn more about her over a cup of coffee as soon as he could pin her down.

CHAPTER 10

Bridgett and Jim had been married only six months when Jim was offered a position with his company at the main plant. He had been working for Richardson Lumber Company most of his life. As a boy, he had started cleaning up after the men finished cutting the logs brought in every day. He worked very hard and soon became an apprentice to one of the men on the line. He was quick at his job and very soon was climbing the ladder to his goal. It was a small village where the company cut its logs, but Jim knew there was a larger plant closer to Boston where the real work was done and he was determined to be there someday.

Bridgett had also lived here all her life and had worked for her parents in their general store as soon as she was big enough to lift the heavy baskets of produce that arrived each day. Since they were able to talk Jim and Bridget had been inseparable so it wasn't a surprise to anyone that as soon as it was permitted, they would marry.

The apartment they lived in was small, but they were together and that was the most important thing in both of their lives. So when Jim was promoted and they found they were to have a house, it looked like all their prayers had been answered. It was a bright sunny morning when Bridgitt, and Jim finished packing up their belongings and set out for their new home. As they pulled out of town, she turned and looked back at the village where she had spent her whole life. She had expected sadness, but instead she felt only joy at a new beginning. Glancing over at Jim, she noticed a faint smile at the corners of his mouth and knew that he too was looking forward to the life ahead of them. We don't have much to put in a house, Bridgitt thought, but with Jim's new job they would be able to furnish it the way they had always dreamed.

In no time at all, they were off the main highway and onto country roads. There was very little traffic and before long even that was gone. It was so peaceful with only the sound of birds and the rustle of corn making it evident they were still awake and not dreaming this whole thing. Bridgitt looked over at Jim and noticed there was a change in him also. It had been weeks since she had seen him looking happy about anything. At first, she thought it might be her fault or that he was sorry they had been married. Then she realized it was something quite different. Something that even he hadn't been able to explain. Now as she watched him driving towards their future, the Jim she knew was back better than before. Perhaps, this new job in the new town was just what he needed. She looked out the side window at the many corn fields around her. How beautiful, she thought. A new beginning. Maybe this is where they could belong.

Suddenly, Bridgitt realized she had been daydreaming again. There was no time for this with all the work to be done on the house. One of her first priorities would be that awful paper in the front hall. It wasn't quite as bad in the bedroom, after all that was the place for roses, wasn't it?

Pinning on her new apron, she started making the house theirs. Opening the curtains, she noticed how close the house was to the one next door. If you leaned out far enough, you could almost tap on the window. She wondered if they were friendly and if she and Jim would fit into the neighbourhood. Dropping the curtain, she looked around her. Well there was plenty of work to do so there wouldn't be much time to neighbour anyway. Just as her curtain fell in place, the curtain on the window next door did the same.

CHAPTER 11

Karen finally finished her shopping and was heading for home. She had decided while she was out she would visit the local decorating centre and see what she could find to replace that awful wallpaper in the hall. Even if she wasn't keeping the house she was sure no one would buy it looking like this. After all, presentation was the key to a sale, they said, whoever they were. There had been more shopping to do than she had anticipated so she was traveling home with a car loaded to the hilt and now had the chore of putting it away. Pulling up the drive, she noticed a new model silver Buick standing in her drive. Not more company. It's worse here in the quiet of the country than it was in the city for visitors. As she pulled up beside the car, she noticed there was no one sitting in it. Also, there was no one on her doorstep. She pulled up just in front of the Buick and opened her door just as a man came around the side of the house. Dan, the man from the pet food aisle. Now what could he want? Returning his wave, she stepped out onto the gravel and started toward him.

"There you are," called Dan. "I thought you might be here earlier so I stopped out to invite you to lunch. However, it looks like we are a bit past that now so I'll invite you to an early dinner. We have a very nice little restaurant just on the other side of the village that will serve just about anything you might desire."

"How nice of you," Karen replied. "I really don't think I can manage it today, however, as I must have bought out half of the village on my first trip and now have to find a place to put everything."

"Not a problem," replied Dan. "Between the two of us we should have everything in its place in no time and still be on time for dinner."

Karen noted the friendly smile on Dan's face and wondered why she hadn't noticed before how good looking he really was. He had an easy, relaxed way of moving and now as he opened the storage area of her car, he seemed far more masculine than he had in the aisle of the grocery store. She had to admit after she left the store, she was sorry they hadn't continued their conversation a bit longer. Then after all how much could you say about dogs when you didn't own one.

"That's very nice of you, but I can't ask you to do that. I have enough stuff in there for a family of five. I can't imagine what I was thinking of buying so much for a two or three week stay. I bought baking supplies and I don't even bake."

She had thought that strange at the time, but in the back of her mind she had been thinking of Jim and how fond he was of her pies. Whoa, there I go again, I haven't baked a pie in my life, and I'm back to Jim. Suddenly, she realized that Dan had unloaded the car and was waiting for her at the door.

"Sorry, here I am daydreaming while you do all the work," she said.

"Not a problem," he replied. "Just open the door and I'll move all this in for you."

Karen fitted the key into the lock and gently pushed the door open. She was aware once more of the fragrance of roses and glanced towards the hall paper. They had certainly been realistic with this paper. Dan entered loaded down with bags.

"That certainly catches the eye doesn't it," he said. "I can see now why I'm carrying so many rolls of wallpaper."

"Yes," said Karen, "it was one of the first things on my to-do list before I show the house. I'm sure no one would get past the door if I left it up. Here let me take some of those bags. The kitchen is just at the end of the hall."

Dan followed Karen down the short hall and through the kitchen door. He found his heart beating just a bit faster. The kitchen was just as he had imagined it all these years. Most of the village boys had at one time or another tried to peek in the windows of what was known as the village haunted house, but the curtains were always pulled so no one had been able to get a glimpse of the inside. Now Dan stood in the kitchen of that house. Carefully, he set the bags on the kitchen table and gazed around the room. Some work had been done to modernize this room, but it still had enough of the old house charm left.

He watched as Karen opened the cupboards and lined the shelves from the bags they had brought in. Could he get a tour of the rest of the house he wondered and how would he go about asking her. There was very little reason for him to see the house on just an invitation to dinner. He wasn't sure he was ready to tell her that he was one of her perspective buyers. Suddenly, he was aware that Karen had been speaking.

"Sorry, I was just admiring your kitchen. What were you saying?"
"I just wondered if you would like a drink before dinner. I think I

would like to freshen up a bit before we go as I've been shopping the better part of the day. The room I believe they called the parlour is livable, no dust covers or cobwebs. You could have your drink in there."

"A drink would be fine," Dan answered. "It would give me a moment to admire more of your wonderful house."

Karen handed the wine bottle and glasses to Dan and made her way up the stairs. Dan turned toward the parlour, wine glasses and bottle in hand. He poured the wine and carefully set them on a side table. Since Karen still hadn't returned, he took advantage of this time to look around. Once again it was just like he had imagined. It was a spacious room with high ceilings. There were two doors leading from the room, one to the dining room and one to the hall. The dining room itself looked large enough to host a dinner party of at least 40. The second door led into the hall with deep rich paneling and a staircase to the upper floors.

The room he was in held the stately bay window that Dan and his friends had tried to peek through as young boys. This was where his dream began. Dan knew then as he strained to see through the heavy curtains that this house would be his someday. It was the only thing that had been constant in his life.

He crossed to the fireplace and picked up a photo of a very pretty girl in an old-fashioned dress. Somehow her face looked familiar. There was a haunted look that seemed to be pulling at him, making him unable to bring his own thoughts back into focus. Suddenly, everything in the room had a familiar feeling, as though he had been here before. Not just as a boy, but something far more real than that. He felt off balance and grasped the mantle.

"There you are," Karen said. "I thought maybe you were having second thoughts about dinner."

Startled, Dan let the photo drop from his fingers to the floor. He heard the frame smash as it made contact with the mantle on the way down.

"Oh," he said. "I am sorry. Look what I've done. I've smashed what must be a family keepsake."

He reached down to pick up the photo just as Karen was reaching for it. There was total silence as their hands brushed. Quickly recovering, Karen slipped the photo into her pocket.

"Nothing to worry about," she said. "It isn't mine, it was here in the house when I arrived. No need to replace it as it will just be cleared out with everything else when the house is sold."

"Seems a shame," said Dan. "It does look very old and probably meant something to someone at one time. If you don't want it, I wouldn't mind taking it. I have a fondness for old things."

Karen slipped her hand over the picture in her pocket. Suddenly, she had a feeling that it was indeed hers. Not willing to give it up, she closed her hand possessively around it. A sudden warmth filled her as if the photo had suddenly known her thoughts and was glad.

"I think for the moment I will hang on to things," she said. "I haven't had time to really look through to see if there are things that belonged to my father. If I do decide to give it up, then of course it will be yours."

Dan had a sudden feeling of loss. "Now that was stupid wasn't it," he thought. Then again, she had looked familiar. Not possible, by the girls' dress, the photo was easily 100 years old. Karen realized they were standing in the parlour without reason.

"If we aren't going to miss dinner as well as lunch, we better have that glass of wine."

Recovering himself, Dan smiled and handed her a glass. "Then I guess we should do just that," he said. Hastily finishing their wine, they made their way down the hall to the front door. It was then Dan had the distinct notion that he could smell roses. Shaking his head, he turned to Karen and smiled. He really was letting his imagination run away with him. It must be the old tale of the haunted house. Surely, he wasn't going to believe them after all this time. As the door closed behind, he just couldn't resist one last look into the hall. As if a wind had suddenly stirred the air, the smell of roses became very strong. It was all he could do to keep from going back into the house to investigate. Shaking his head to clear the fragrance, he decided it was time to put his boyhood behind him along with all the silly notions about this house. After all, he thought if he was going to buy the house, he had to put those ghosts to bed. He was unaware of a voice as he shut the door behind him and made his way down the steps to Karen and the evening ahead.

CHAPTER 12

The house next door was quiet with very little light from the windows. The only show of life was the curtain flutter in the downstairs room better known as the study. This was not unusual as it was the owner's habit of sitting at this window watching. Both houses had been sitting side by side for over 100 years sharing the same ground roots until they had almost become one. Also, sharing life.

Edna felt like the protector of both houses as she too had been here for almost 100 years. She remembered all the stories connected with her neighbours house, the true ones and the made-up ones. She wondered what the village would think if they knew how close one was to the other. As a child living here, she remembered the hate. There had been a time when the villagers believed that all new people settling there were witches and used any means to send them away, any means at all.

She sat by the window tonight thinking of the young woman who had recently arrived next door. At first, she thought that the house had been sold and felt quite safe. The house had been empty for many years. It had sold twice in her lifetime, but the new owners never moved in, and it was put up for sale again. There had never been a good feeling about that house, and finally, it was left to its own with only a groundskeeper to look out for its welfare. Now it was occupied again and her niece had informed her that the woman was related to the original owners. So, it was to start all over, she thought, and once more she must take her stand as she had for so many years before.

CHAPTER 13

The sun was golden yellow and the grass seemed greener, wet with dew. Joe unpacked his tools from the back of his truck and stood for a moment taking in the morning and the smell of lilacs. Soon they would be gone and another fragrance would take over in their place, but he always felt the lilacs were the best first thing in the morning. With a stretch, he braced himself for the day. It seemed that the weeds just waited for him to leave every day and then take over the gardens just in spite.

He followed around the side of the house to the rear patio where he would spend his morning mulching the roses. There was always an area to work as most of the flowers and shrubs were planted for a constant flow of colour. He had tended the house for most of his life and had planted all of the garden himself aside from the roses that had been put in by the original owner. He wondered if the new owner would keep him on. Well, no point standing around wondering, just get on with it before the sun was too hot to work in this area. As he was about to pour the fertilizer on the bed, he heard the side door open. Pulling his hat off and wiping his hands on his overalls, he prepared to meet his new boss.

CHAPTER 14

Karen had been wondering when she would cross paths with her caretaker. It had been three days since she arrived and all she had seen of him was a fast glimpse as he left in his truck each morning. Sometimes it seemed as though he wasn't really there, and the gardens were tending themselves. When she thought about it, many of the things happening didn't seem too real. The roses for example, not just the ones in the garden but in the hallway and on her bedroom walls. Even now as she hurried to dress, she had a feeling of being too close to the walls even at two feet away. The smell of roses, sometimes was so overpowering it made her light headed.

Turning to the window with thought of opening it, she noticed Joe in the rose garden. He was about to start his work and she might be able to talk to him before he got away again. Slipping into the rest of her clothes, she hurried down the stairs and out the side door.

"Good morning," she said brightly and held out her hand to her caretaker. "I decided it was about time we met as you have been taking care of my property all these years, and I didn't even know you existed let alone the property until recently. Did you work for my father when he lived here?"

"Sorry miss," Joe replied, "but I never met your father and this house has been empty for as long as I can remember. I was just a young boy when I was hired to look after the yards, and no one has lived in the house in all that time. The real estate company in town pays me to keep the yards tended and make sure that a cleaning crew comes once a month to clean the house."

"You mean that no one has lived here since you were a boy?"

Karen asked.

"That's right miss, no one in all those years."

That was strange Karen thought, why would her father own a house and never live in it.? "Did you know the people who owned it before my father?" she asked.

"No miss, like I said I was just a boy when the real estate company hired me and the house was empty then."

How strange, Karen thought. Had her father bought an empty house and then left it for someone else to care for? Maybe there was something structurally wrong, and the house was not livable. If so, it meant she would be stuck with it herself. She would have to make friends with Joe. He could probably tell her who to get in touch with for the information. She turned her attention back to Joe.

"I was just going to have a cup of coffee," she said. "Would you come in and join me?" Joe mopped his head with the red bandana he had pulled from his overall pocket. "That would be nice about now."

"Well come along, it should be ready. I might even find something sweet to go with it."

"Joe stopped in his tracks and suddenly looked troubled. "In the house you mean, Miss?" "Of course, in the house," Karen replied. "Oh, don't worry about your work clothes, I'm sure there is nothing you can hurt in the kitchen."

"Oh no, Miss," he said, "I couldn't come in the house, out here would be just fine."

"I wouldn't think of it, you will come into the kitchen and sit with me."

Karen noticed that Joe had suddenly become very pale and was backing away from her. What on earth could she have done to frighten him, for that is what he appeared to be, very frightened.

"Thank you miss, but I can't come into the house. I have never been in the house."

"You have never been in the house," Karen asked in surprise? "All these years you have worked here, but have never been in the house? How do you know if the cleaning has been done if you don't check on the workers," she asked?

"They are good people," Joe replied, "and I never have to check on them. I know they will always do what needs to be done. Now Miss, if you don't need anything further, I will be leaving. I have other grounds to keep, and I am already late."

With this, he hurried to his truck and before it was hardly in gear raced up the driveway and was soon out of sight. The unattended rose garden left behind.

"What about your coffee," Karen called. But Joe was too far up the lane to hear her. From the house next door, the curtain in the library fluttered closed.

CHAPTER 15

After her unpleasant meeting with Joe, Karen decided it was a good day to go through the house and see just what her father had left her. Until today, she had been too busy stocking the cupboards and shopping for wallpaper to pay much attention to the rest of the house. Picking up her cup of coffee, she started up the stairs to the second floor. There were two other bedrooms besides her own and a full bath. Also, there was a small door at the end on the left that she assumed was to the attic, another level up. From the back of the house, you could just see a small window under the eaves hidden by the ivy.

She would start there working from the top of the house to the bottom. She had to admit she wasn't too thrilled at entering the attic or the basement. They had been frightening places for her from the time she was a child. Making her way down the hall, she paused for a moment at each door. Nothing out of the ordinary. The other two bedrooms were furnished much like her own except for the rose wallpaper. These rooms were more ordinary and subdued in their décor. She had already seen the bath and although it was very old fashioned, it too was decorated on the plain side. This would probably make it easier to sell when she was ready, and she would only have to deal with the one bedroom on this floor.

She approached the door to the attic and with some hesitation took hold of the doorknob. Why was it she wondered that most attic doors were made smaller and stairs more steep than regular ones? Maybe this was a way to keep people out. Well, she wasn't about to stop now. Opening the door, she started up the narrow stairway. The stairs were so steep she felt like she was leaning backwards every step.

At the top, she found herself in a very dirty room. She could see that the small window was not only covered with vines on the outside, but with years of grime on the inside. Apparently, the cleaning staff didn't venture this far. To the left of the stairs was another small door. She carefully made her way through the semi dark and tried the handle. Locked, of course it would be, why would she think differently? There must be a key somewhere. Possibly, over the door frame where many past generations left them as though no one would think to look there. However, these people had not been so trusting there was nothing there.

Her eyes were becoming more accustomed to the light, and she could see that there was nothing in the attic but dust. She would have to search for a key later. She really needed to know what was behind the door before she listed the house.

Turning, she made her way down the stairs. Halfway down, she was suddenly aware of a sound coming from the room above her and the overpowering smell of roses. There was a tightening in her chest and it became hard to breathe; she felt herself slipping down the steps, then nothing but darkness. Just as the dark enfolded her, she was sure a hand held her from falling down the rest of the way and then there was nothing.

CHAPTER 16

Dan hadn't been able to get Karen off his mind all day. They had in just a short time become more than friends and for the first time he could remember the house was not the most important thing in his life. He still wanted to buy it, but now he kept seeing Karen in it and in his life. He realized he knew very little about her. They had talked in great length about their families but nothing that really told him about her.

Sitting here in his office, he knew that what he wanted most was to go home every evening after work and find her waiting for him. For Dan, this was as first as he had taken most relationships in the past as just a pastime with no future involved. Still he knew that his future was with her. Noting the time, he decided that he couldn't do much more for today so he closed up the case he was working on and prepared to leave. Now he realized he was the only one left in the office.

He vaguely remembered Jeff sticking his head in the door and saying good night and the office secretary asking if he needed her to stay and then nothing. Switching off his light and pulling the door closed behind him, he walked out into the dusk.

As he pulled away from the parking lot, he found he was once again thinking of Karen. He wondered what she might be doing at this hour and thinking of possibly another dinner date. On a whim, he made the turn that led to her house and started up the lane. As he pulled in front, he found Karen's car stopped at the steps. He glanced in as he passed and saw she had left her car keys in the ignition. Not a great idea even if the village was reasonably safe. He reached in for them and found she had also left her day's purchases on the seat. Strange he thought, picking up the parcels. Possibly, the phone rang and she just forgot to come back out for them.

As he approached the front door, he found that it too had been left ajar. Opening the door slightly, he called Karen's name. When there was no answer, he pushed the door open and entered the hall. Making his way through the house, he found no one on the main floor. He called her name again and still no answer. As his foot touched the first step, there was an overpowering smell of roses, and Dan took a hold of the banister for balance. It was as though the fragrance was holding him back from going upstairs. Frightened at the thought of what might have happened to Karen, he fought his way to the second floor. It took all the willpower he could muster. When he reached the top, he was suddenly unable to go on. He struggled to overcome the feeling and finally dropping to his knees, he broke free.

It was then he saw Karen lying on the floor at the end of the hall at the attic door. He pushed his way forward and kneeling beside her checked for a pulse. There was one, although slight she seemed to be breathing normally. He breathed a sigh of relief and as if she was aware, he was there she opened her eyes. Dan, she thought, why is he here and what am I doing on the floor? I must have fallen the last few steps coming down from the attic. As she started to sit up, Dan gently pushed her back.

"Not yet," he said. "We had better make sure nothing is broken or there are no bumps that need tending."

"I'm sure there aren't," Karen said. "I can't imagine what happened. One minute I was stepping down and the next, I woke up and saw you."

She pushed herself up on one elbow and carefully moved all her limbs to make sure nothing had broken in the fall. Dan took her hand and slowly helped her to her feet.

"I think we should go downstairs and fix you a good strong drink," he said.

Karen started slowly down the hall with Dan supporting her. She wondered how long she had been lying there before Dan arrived. It wasn't like her to be so clumsy, but then she had become a lot of different things since she came to this house. As a rule, she was well organized and knew exactly where she was going, but she felt vague and disoriented. It had to be the new surroundings and that she was all alone. Even though several people had befriended her, it wasn't like the old friends back home. Back home. Somehow, she felt it was slipping away from her, and she would never get it back. Taking the drink Dan handed her, she settled down in the study to take stock.

Dan sat next to Karen on the couch. She looked very pale, he thought, but then she had just fallen down the stairs. He assumed she had fallen down the stairs as she was lying at the foot when he found her. He tried to remember what she had said to him as she was coming to. Yes, she did say she had fallen down the last few stairs, but the door was closed and she was lying across it. How could she have closed the door?

He was aware that the house had suddenly become very dark and a chill ran down his spine. The smell of roses became so strong that he felt as though he would smother. Fearfully, he glanced over at Karen. She had suddenly become very still and staring straight ahead. It was as if she was in another room and in another place that only she could see. He reached forward and touched her arm, but there was still no movement. Standing, he took hold of her shoulders and shook her until she focused on him. With a start, Karen looked up at Dan as if for the first time.

"Dan, what are you doing here?"

"I've been here for the past half hour," he said. "I made you the drink you're holding."

Karen stared blankly at the drink in her hand. When did she get that, she wondered, and why couldn't she remember Dan making it?

CHAPTER 17

Joe had been working in the garden all morning. He didn't feel comfortable here anymore. He had spent most of his life in these gardens, but now everything seemed different. He liked the new owner and felt that he should talk to her about the history of her house. Not that he believed all the tales that spread through the village. He knew that some of the older families had used the stories to keep their young in line, but they were after all just old stories and nothing to be afraid of. Still it wouldn't do any harm just to fill the young owner in on the old tales of the house and also on the ones that the village today still believed.

He realized young Luke, the part time boy who helped out with errands and raking for him was working on the other side of the hedge, still Joe suddenly felt as if he was alone. Although he could see no one, he felt that there was a presence with him and he longed to finish up and be on his way. He could hear Luke humming to himself. He must have those earphones on again. It seemed like the whole younger generation walked around with plugs in their ears. Not like when he was a boy, he thought. Things surely had changed.

A sudden chill ran across his back and he turned expecting to see someone behind him, but there was no one there. Once again, he had the overpowering scent of roses. This was not the side of the house where the roses were planted. How could the scent be so strong here? Also, he could no longer hear Luke and the sky had clouded over. It seemed more like evening instead of early afternoon. He reached to set down his shears but found he could no longer move from the spot. Fear set in when he could not call out for help as the darkening clouds settled around him.

Joe glanced up at the bedroom window hoping that Karen was looking out. Yes, there was someone there just behind the curtains. She would have to see him and come to help. He could feel his heart pounding, and he could no longer breathe. Why wasn't she coming to help him? He knew she could see him and knew he was in trouble and yet she still just stood looking down at him. Luke must know too as he wouldn't hear the shears and would wonder why Joe had stopped working. Then he realized that Luke couldn't hear him because of those damn earphones. There was only one who could help. He glanced once again at the upstairs window and saw immediately that it wasn't Karen standing there but a woman he did know. It was then he knew that he should have warned Karen about the house for she was surely in danger. He also knew that it was too late for that now and as he slowly slipped into the dark, he prayed that someone else would take over and save her.

CHAPTER 18

Karen slowly unlocked the front door. She had spent most of the day in the sheriff's office answering questions. She was still somewhat in shock about the death of her gardener. It had started out a pleasant morning with sun shining and the sound of Joe and his young helper working in the garden. She thought later she just might take out some lemonade and cookies to them. As she went to the cupboard to check her cookie supply, she was aware that Joe had stopped his trimming. This might be the time for them to take a break.

Placing the glasses and plate of cookies on a tray, she headed for the side yard. She could hear the noise of brush being stacked on the other side of the hedge but still no sound from Joe. Peeking around, she saw a slight young boy picking up the branches that Joe had cut. He seemed to be keeping time somehow as he brought the cuttings to the bag. It was then she noticed the earphones and realized he was keeping time to the music he was hearing. Moving slowly, she worked her way around in front of him. Luke noticed her and pulled the earphones from his ears. Stepping forward, Karen introduced herself and offered him a drink and asked where Joe was.

Luke now was aware that Joe was no longer cutting the hedge on the other side. He wondered when he had stopped and why he hadn't said something. It wasn't like Joe not to check on his work, and he wondered how long it had been since he and Joe had talked. Working his way around the side of the hedge, he called out but there was no answer. That was strange, Joe wouldn't have left without telling him.

As he walked up the hedge, he noticed a foot sticking out a bit further up the garden. He thought Joe must have found something under the hedge that could not be cut by shears and was clipping it out by hand. He turned to call out to Karen and realized she was right behind him. He pointed to what he thought were Joe's feet just ahead. Both Karen and Luke called out again, but still no answer. Karen suddenly felt a cold chill run down her spine. Why didn't Joe answer them? He had to hear them calling. Fear made her put her hand on Luke's shoulder to stop the boy from going any further. She handed him the tray and told him to wait.

Stepping forward, she realized she had been right to be frightened. As she came closer, she could see that the feet sticking out of the hedge were indeed Joe's. She could also see there was no movement coming from him. Parting the branches, she looked down into the sightless eyes of her gardener.

He had become wedged between the branches as he fell so his head was twisted at a right angle from the rest of his body. Karen gasped at the sight of him and stepped back into the path. Seeing Luke starting forward, she held up a hand for him to stay back. Even though she knew there was no chance he was alive she reached for Joe's wrist for a pulse. She knew then there was nothing they could do. Taking the tray, she sent Luke on to the sheriff's office to get help.

Now she was home again. Leaning back against the door, she stood for a moment thinking about what had happened. The time at the sheriff's office had been tiring, and she could barely stand. The sheriff told her he would get back to her after the autopsy and that she should not leave town. This alone puzzled her as she had not been there when Joe died, and she was sure it had to be a heart attack. After all, he was not a young man, and he had been doing rather physical work for such a warm day. She just had gone out with a drink to have them take a break. Now life had become part of a very bad mystery story. Slowly, she sank to the floor. She was so tired. She would just rest here while she tried to puzzle things out.

Karen laid her head against the entrance wall and closed her eyes. She found the silence of the house soothing after her long

Or deal. The scent of roses filled the air and worked like a sedation for her. Slowly, she ran her fingers over the worn carpet on the bottom step of the staircase. It was an old habit of hers when she was tired. Her fingers would worry the smallest thread of whatever she was near until it became loose in her hand.

Suddenly, she was aware of something hard beneath the thread. Coming to a sitting position, she went back over the rug until she found the spot once more. She moved the item little by little until she had worked it out from under the rug. She found in her hand a small gold key.

Now what door does this open she wondered. She had keys to all the doors in the house and had opened each one. Even the basement, although she hadn't ventured down there yet as even from the top of the stairs, it looked foreboding. This key was somewhat different from the other house keys, and she wondered if it even belonged to the house. Then she remembered the door in the attic. The one place she hadn't been. She puzzled a moment longer over the key then decided to try it later. Not now. She'd had too many puzzles for one day. Slipping the key back into her pocket, she leaned back against the wall.

CHAPTER 19

Sheriff Hennessey pushed his chair back from the desk. He had been sitting puzzling over the details of old Joe's death. He had spent the better half of the morning with the new owner of the old house and young Luke Jones. Luke had come running into his office babbling something about an accident, and he had followed him back to the garden where he found old Joe lying in the hedge. The owner, Karen, was kneeling beside him as if trying to bring him around. At first sight, he knew that it was too late to help. Old Joe was lying on his back, his head contorted in an odd position as if looking over his shoulder.

He checked the body for signs of a fall, but there was no sign of blood or even bruising on the body. He knew Joe was in top physical shape in spite of his age, for he had been in the doctor's office just the week before when Joe had been in for his yearly physical. He remembered the doctor commenting on the shape he was in and asking what his secret was. "Clean living," Joe replied, and both he and the doctor had a laugh about this as they knew Joe liked to tip more than a few every week-end.

Tipping his chair back and propping his feet up on his desk, he turned his mind back to the house. It had always been a problem. Because it was empty, he was constantly chasing young bucks off the property. It seemed the best place in the village for them to take their girls for a good scare before enticing them into the back seat of their cars. Also, there were many tales surrounding the house at the time of the witch hunts It had even been rumoured that one had lived in the house and that when the people of the village went to find her, she magically disappeared before their eyes. Some said that was the day a spell was put on old Joe turning his hair grey and tying him to the house forever.

He had heard all the stories and the more he heard the more outlandish they became. Joe was responsible for many of them himself. He even told about how the widow next door was also tied to the house and had to watch over it until the witch returned to take out her revenge on all the families of the people who had condemned her. With a sigh, Sheriff Hennessey lowered his feet to the floor. He knew there would be trouble in the village now. People would be frightened when they thought about the old tales and his phone would be ringing off the desk.

He better drive out and warn the new owner that she might have a few visitors and let her know he was there for her. He unlocked his desk drawer and took out his gun. It had been a long time since he felt the need to do this. Shoving his hat on his head, he went out stopping in the outer office to tell his deputy where he could be reached then made his way to the parking lot and his car.

Luke stood in the garden looking at old Joe's feet sticking out from under the bushes. He had gone for the sheriff as the new owner Karen had told him and then came back with the sheriff to see what had happened. All the way to the house in the sheriff's car he kept remembering the look on Joe's face. He had never seen a dead person before, but he knew for sure that Joe was dead. He couldn't understand why. Joe had seemed fine when they started work this morning and now he is dead. Luke had his headset on and was working on the other side of the hedge so he couldn't be sure that someone hadn't come into the yard and killed Joe. He watched as the sheriff covered Joe's body and questioned Karen. He had told the sheriff all he knew on the way over from the office and now he stood his earphone hanging loosely around his neck idly waiting to be told he could leave.

Glancing at the house, his eyes lifted to the window looking down where Joe had fallen. There was a slight movement of the curtain and for a moment, Luke stood very still, eyes transfixed. Then slowly he turned and walked away.

CHAPTER 20

Edna had become very frightened. She had been listening to the sound of Joe's shears as he clipped away at his bushes. This was the day that the boy Luke joined him doing a real clean up job of the gardens next door. Now all she heard was a rustle of leaves and twigs as Luke picked up after Joe. He wouldn't just go and leave Luke to finish on his own. Noticing the time on the mantle clock, she realized it was far too soon for Joe to finish for the day. She gently pulled back the sheer curtains and peered out. Yes, there was Luke picking up close to her side of the fence and as usual he had earphones settled tightly to his head. She leaned further into the glass for a better look. Joe was nowhere in sight. Edna pulled the curtain open wide and looked in the opposite direction.

There just at the end of the hedge, she could see what looked like an arm sticking through the brambles. She felt her heart start to pound as she realized the arm was covered with a blue sleeve the very colour of the shirt that Joe always wore. Frightened for him, she tapped on the window glass to attract the boy's attention. When he did not respond, she tried again harder this time. Still nothing, it had to be those blasted earphones that all the young were wearing today. They became totally unaware of the world around them. She was just about to tap again when she noticed a movement in the upper window.

Stepping back so as not to be seen, she took her binoculars from the shelf and put them to her eyes. Yes, there was movement up there; it must be Karen the new owner. Surely, she would notice Joe and come to help him. Another movement just below the window attracted her attention, and she stepped further back into the room. Peering once again through the glasses, she spotted Karen as she made her way towards Joe. With a quick flick, she raised her glasses once again to the shadow in the window. As if they became aware of her watching the figure fade in the shadows but just before they did, the figure looked across the hedge into Edna's eyes. Dropping the glasses to the floor, she pressed herself against the wall. This couldn't be true she thought as she pressed her hand against her heart. It was starting again. Edna knew there would be trouble, great trouble for Edna had seen a figure from the past.

CHAPTER 21

Dan sped up the lane to Karen's house. He had been tied up all day and hadn't heard about Joe until just a half hour ago. He had been so preoccupied with thinking about buying the house that he had neglected his business for the past two days and decided to spend his day behind closed doors catching up. Now as he jumped from the car, he realized that when Karen had needed him most he had not been there. He rushed up the steps and knocked on the door. As if she had been waiting on the other side, the door opened and Karen stumbled into his arms. Karen couldn't stop the flow of tears when she saw Dan.

"I thought you weren't coming," she cried. "It was awful. It was hot, and I was on my way out with something for them to drink. I couldn't see Joe so I went around the hedge to find the boy. He couldn't hear me at first as he was listening to his music. When I finally got his attention, he came with me around the hedge and that was when we found Joe. The minute I looked at him, he had such a look of fear on his face like he had seen a ghost. He wasn't sick Dan, everyone said that and still he died. What could have made him afraid? "What could have been so bad that it would frighten him to death?"

Dan held Karen for a moment longer, then steered her into the living room. Sitting her down on the couch, he went to the bar and poured her a generous shot of brandy. "Here, drink this," he said, "it will steady you."

As Karen sipped at the drink, she reached for Dan's hand. "How," she asked, "could someone just die from fear?"

Dan turned her to face him. "It may have seemed that way only because you were frightened yourself at the time. You have to remember Joe was old, and it was a very hot day to be working in the garden. It was more than likely just from the heat."

Karen took another sip of her drink. It did make sense what Dan said. The temperature had soared today, one of the hottest days this year the news had reported. It did seem the logical answer since Karen had not found anything in the garden that might frighten anyone. The boy had also seemed calm enough until they found the body, so the logical reason would be the heat. She leaned back against Dan's shoulder and finished her drink. She knew she could count on Jim to be there when she needed him. They were so happy in their new home. Everything would be alright now. Jim? Who was Jim?

CHAPTER 22

Edna couldn't move from the spot. She was afraid if she looked out the window she would still see the figure next door. It couldn't be happening again. The house had been empty for so long that she thought she could finally relax. Then today happened, Joe, poor old Joe. She had watched him most of the morning trimming his beloved hedges as if they were his children. Joe had always been so proud of the gardens. He had been the caretaker most of his life just as Edna had been the watcher. There had been no choice for either of them. They had been young at the time they were put in charge of the house, and both knew that it could be for the rest of their lives.

They were the keepers of the secret that the village and the house held. Everything had been quiet for such a long time until Karen had come to the house. Edna had hoped that the few things she had seen with her glasses had been just her imagination playing tricks on her until today. When looking up into the upstairs window of the house, she had come face to face with Bridgitt O'Hara.

CHAPTER 23

Shelby trudged up the steps to the front door. She hadn't been back to the house since the first day when Karen had taken her on a preliminary tour. She thought at the time that Karen wasn't in any hurry to sell so she had left her to think things over for a few days. However, now with the death of Joe she might want to unload the property in a hurry. She rang the doorbell and waited. She could hear the bell resounding through the house but no other noise within. Just my luck, she thought, to drive all the way out here and then find there was no one home.

She thought about calling Jeff to check on their dinner date for that night but realized he had left a message earlier on her answering machine saying he had to be out of town on business for the next week and would call her when he returned. This was a bit annoying for she had intended on pinning him down at dinner about where their relationship was going from here.

They had been a thing for so many years that many in the village thought they were already married. Now she decided it was the time to make their relationship more permanent. It was just as much her fault as she had been happy enough living her own independent life. Well, that would be over when he got back. It was time she knew where her life was going from here.

She could visit her aunt next door so the trip wouldn't be a total loss. She shuddered a bit at the thought of this. Her aunt had never been one of her favorite people, but she would leave a sizable inheritance when she died. For this reason and this alone, Shelby made a point of visiting at least once a month just to keep her presence known. She rang the bell once more and still hearing no movement, she tried the door knob.

What luck it wasn't locked.

"Hello," she called, "anyone home?" Pushing the door open wide and calling once again, she stepped into the front hallway. "Karen it's Shelby," she called, still no answer. She wondered if she dared take a further peek at the house, for sale purposes only, she told herself. Pondering for only a minute, she shut the door behind her and started through the house.

Pulling out her notebook, she once again took notes on the downstairs area. Most of the rooms looked good enough, she thought. It looked like Karen had started on some minor repairs in the preparation for sale. At least, the house was clean. Coming back into the hall, Shelby was once again caught up in the rose wallpaper. That would definitely have to go before she showed the house. It seemed even more overpowering than it had on her first visit.

She picked her way up the stairs and started her notes on the bedrooms and the bathroom. Everything looked presentable here as well. One bedroom door was locked, and Shelby decided that Karen must be using this one as temporary storage. Moving down the hall, she found another small door she hadn't noticed on her first visit. Opening the door, she found a narrow staircase leading up to another floor. This must be the attic. Of course, there would be one. She just hadn't thought about it on her first trip. She had better take a look as sometimes an attic or basement could ruin a sale.

The stairs were hardly wide enough to hold a foot so she had to pick her way slowly and carefully to the top. When she reached the top, she found herself in a large empty room with a small door at the far end. The only window was very small and dirty making the room very gloomy. Making her way across the room she tried the door handle. Locked. One more room, she thought. She would ask Karen to open them so she could have a full picture of her sale. A sudden breeze stirred the dust at Shelby's feet and chilled the air, and she was suddenly afraid. She had turned to make her way down the stairs when she spied a large trunk in the corner just off the staircase. Her curiosity was too keen not to at least take a look. It was an old-fashioned trunk with large hinges and wide leather straps. She struggled with the lock for some minutes until it finally gave way and the lid flew open. Shelby peered inside. Nothing much here except a few old clothes and what looked like an old journal. Reaching down for the book, she was suddenly aware of movement behind her. Before she could turn to see what or who it was, she felt strong hands on her back. There was nothing to hold onto and she found herself falling headlong into the trunk.

Before she was able to pull herself up, the trunk lid closed trapping her inside. She heard the lock snap shut and the straps being tightened. She began to hammer on the lid of the trunk, but there was no way she could push it open. Footsteps on the stairs told her she was being left alone up here with no help in sight. She struggled and called out for help until she had no voice left. The dust settled once again on the attic floor and the muted light from the window darkened until there was nothing left in the attic but an old trunk and silence.

CHAPTER 24

Karen had no sooner closed the front door when she heard a car in the driveway. That must be Dan, she thought as he was picking her up for dinner, and it was almost time. Just as she touched the door handle the doorbell rang.

With a smile on her face, she threw open the door and was about to comment on how punctual Dan was when she realized it wasn't Dan but a delivery man holding a bulky parcel under his arm.

"Karen Warren," he asked?

"Yes," she replied.

"Delivery from Boston," he said, "and I need you to sign for it." Karen took the clipboard the man offered and began to sign on the specified line. Now, who would be sending her a parcel from Boston she wondered? Not many of her friends really knew where she was as she had originally thought she would be gone for only a few days. That thought had run into weeks and still she had no immediate plans to leave. Thanking the man, she closed the door and looked down at the parcel in her hands.

Dropping her purse in the hallway, she made her way back to the kitchen for scissors to cut the string that held the parcel together. As she set it on the table, she noticed the return address was from her lawyer's office. Probably more papers to sign in her father's estate. She hoped this would soon be over, and she could return to her own life. Setting the parcel aside, she filled the kettle to boil. She would face the paperwork over a cup of tea. Kicking off her shoes, she snipped the string dumping everything onto the kitchen table. It had been double wrapped, and she found inside a packet of letters and what appeared to be a small black journal.

It was very old and Karen was sure she had never seen it in her father's things. She lifted the packet of letters and found they, too, were very old. There was something very familiar about the hand writing. She knew it was not her mother or father's hand but she felt she had seen it before. Setting the letters aside, she opened the journal to the front page. It was beautiful old script, and someone had taken great care in writing it. The paper was yellow with age, and she took it to the window for better light. She could just make out a name on the front leaf, Jim O'Hara. This name was familiar too. Karen was sure she had either read it or heard it mentioned somewhere

Setting both the letters and journal aside, she picked up the single sheet of paper with the lawyer's letterhead. Dear Karen, it read. While finishing up your father's estate, I came across these things that I think you should have. There's a sealed letter included that was to be given to you on his death, but only after you were informed about the house. I am sending it on to you in case there is something you will need in the sale of the house. If there is anything further I can do for you regarding this or any other matter, don't hesitate to call me. Cordially yours.

Karen picked up the envelope with her father's handwriting and held it for a few minutes just looking at it. It seemed like only yesterday that her father was sitting at his desk writing. She wondered if this was one of the things he was writing at the time. Sliding the tip of a kitchen knife on the fold, she opened the letter. She sat at the table and started to read.

Dear Karen. If you are reading this letter, then I am gone and you already know about the house. Many times over the years, I was going to tell you about it, but I never could get up the courage to do so. I have sent along your great grandmother's journal. I think when you read this, it will explain everything. It will also tell you why I have kept the house a secret all these years.

Karen had been so engrossed in her reading that she jumped when she heard a car horn. That would be Dan picking her up for dinner. She also hadn't noticed that the tea kettle was boiling over, and she rushed to turn it off. Taking the letters and journal, she stuffed them in the kitchen cupboard. They would have to wait until later, she thought and headed for the front door. Had she been more aware, she might have noticed as she closed the front door behind her, a deep sigh and a slight rustle of roses.

CHAPTER 25

Finally, Jeff was back from his business trip. Jeff had been waiting for Shelby for over an hour. He had left a message at Shelby's to meet him at the coffee shop for lunch. He hadn't seen her since his return from his business trip and thought she would be happy to see him. He also hinted at a week-end away together just to sweeten the pot. So, where was she?

He knew that Shelby was going to try to pin him down to a serious relationship this week-end, and he wondered how he really felt about this. They had been dating off and on since high school but lately it had become a bit more serious. He wasn't sure he was ready to settle down, but then he wasn't sure he was ready to give Shelby up either. She had become a part of his life in a way, and he couldn't imagine not having her around. Maybe it was time to settle down.

Glancing at his watch once again, he was surprised to see that she was now an hour and a half late. Jeff was used to being kept waiting by Shelby as she always had one more client to call or one more house to photograph. However, it was the week-end, and she had been excited over their trip and had promised to be on time. Maybe she was tied up with something at home.

He opened his cell phone and dialed her number. After four rings, Shelby's voice came on saying she could not be reached until the following Tuesday. He hung up and dialed her office. The only difference there was the wording in the message. She wasn't there. Where could she be? He decided maybe he should check out her apartment in case something had happened to her. Tucking his phone in his pocket, he started out of the mall towards his car. Not like her at all. He would have to pin the sheriff down and insist he try harder to find her.

He had a bad feeling since it was not in her character for her to act this way. She was always eager about any of their dates and was usually waiting for him. He felt a slight shiver as all of a sudden; he thought there might be something very wrong.

CHAPTER 26

Sheriff Hennessey puzzled over the report in his hand. It had been five days now since the disappearance of Shelby Thorton. The last she had been seen was when she took off in her car to check on the Warren property. No one had actually seen her head that way, but when she left the office, she told the secretary that she was going to see if Karen was ready to list the house. There were no other appointments on her desk calendar so it was assumed she was just going to be working this property at the moment. Who could tell with Shelby as she was always changing her mind midstream if something more interesting came along.

Daily he had a call from Jeff Lewis wanting to know if he made any headway on finding Shelby, and why hadn't he brought more men in to look for her. He understood Jeff being upset as he and Shelby had been a thing since school. He wondered why they hadn't married before now. He expected it was just cold feet on Jeff's part. However, now that he couldn't reach Shelby, he just might decide it was time to settle down. Sheriff Hennesey hoped he would find her soon so Jeff would give him a rest. Sighing, he dropped his feet to the floor and stood up. Taking his hat from the rack behind the door and tightening his tie, he headed out to the reception desk to let them know where he could be reached. After picking up his messages, he climbed into his jeep and pulled away. This was not going to be easy, he thought, for Karen had been here just a short time and already had been involved in one tragic incident. Not that Shelby could be a tragic incident but he had a gut feeling that she hadn't just driven away without at least leaving a message at her office.

He could feel something in the air, something he had felt before but had slipped it to the back of his mind. Stop, he thought, no use dwelling on something that might never happen or borrowing trouble before it happened. He turned up the lane to the Warren house. There was something ominous about this house, he thought. Slowly, he drove up the lane and stopped at the front door. Karen's car was parked in the drive. Good, he thought, at least she is home and I can get this over with.

Karen was busy in the kitchen putting away the few groceries she had picked up when she heard a car in the front drive. She closed the cupboard door and headed for the front hall. I do hope it isn't that real estate woman, I don't think I could handle her this afternoon. She opened the door to the sheriff standing on her porch. His hand still extended to ring the bell. "Sheriff, how nice to see you," Karen said. "I do hope this is a social call."

"Good afternoon, Miss Warren. No, not really a social call. May I come in?

"Certainly," Karen replied. "How rude of me. I guess I was just surprised to see you. I half expected it to be Shelby Thorton from the real estate office, and I wasn't looking forward to an afternoon with her."

"Now, why would that be," the sheriff asked.

"Oh, nothing really," Karen replied. "It's just that she can be a bit wearing, and I do have the start of a headache. Somehow, Shelby and headaches don't seem to mix. I'm just about to have a cup of coffee, would you join me?"

"Yes, I think I might do that," he replied.

He followed Karen into the kitchen. It was more modern than he thought it would be as no one had lived in the house for many years. Someone had gone to the trouble of putting in modern plumbing and equipment as though they were planning on staying. He knew Karen had not equipped the house as there had been no contractors from the village hired to do so.

He watched as Karen poured the coffee and set out cream and sugar. She seemed calm, he thought, not like someone who had something to hide. She was either a good actress or did not know about Shelby's disappearance. Karen set the coffee out on the kitchen table. She wondered why the sheriff was paying her a visit as she had told him all she could about the death of Old Joe. Judging by his expression, it was a serious visit so she took a chair opposite him and waited for him to start.

"I suppose you know about the disappearance of Shelby Thorton," he said. "She has been missing for five days now, and no one seems to know where she might have gone. I thought you might have some knowledge as the last known place she was coming to was yours. Possibly she mentioned a trip she might be taking when she talked to you."

Karen's look was one of surprise. This was the first she had heard about Shelby being missing. True she had called a few days ago and said she was going to be out this way and would drop in, but there had been no appointment made at the time and she had told Shelby that she was having second thoughts about selling the house.

"I never saw her, Sheriff," she said. "She may have come out this way, but I have been so busy running back and forth to the village for supplies that I could easily have missed her. It seems strange that she would not let her office know exactly where she was going to be in case they needed her for anything."

"Well, she did tell her office her destination. She told them she was coming out to talk to you about selling your house."

"I'm sorry," Karen said, "but she never arrived."

"Well, I guess that's another dead end," the sheriff said, putting down his coffee cup and getting to his feet. "Thank you for your time and the coffee. Maybe I'll make a trip next door and see if her aunt can help at all."

Karen saw the sheriff to the front hall. As she opened the door, the sheriff turned to look at the staircase. "I noticed you still have the old wallpaper.

"Jake at the hardware store told me you bought new paper right after you arrived. Thought maybe it was for this old hall."

"Yes, I did, but I haven't had the time to do anything about it. Besides I find the old paper grows on you after a while. I may just leave it there."

The sheriff picked up his hat and prepared to leave. "Once again, thanks for the coffee and I'll be on my way." Karen closed the door behind him. She watched as he made his way to his car. He stopped for a moment and glanced at the upstairs window with a puzzled look on his face. Then crawling into his car, turned up the lane. Turning, Karen leaned against the front door. She glanced up the staircase into the upstairs hall. It seemed very dark for this time of day, and the smell of roses was almost overpowering. Once again, she had second thoughts about the paper. She really must do something about it, but not today. Checking the drive once more, she turned and made her way back to the kitchen.

She picked up the coffee cups and set them in the sink to wash later. Her headache had subsided, possibly knowing Shelby would not be coming today. Standing, looking out the kitchen windows she thought how beautiful the country was. It seemed to stretch for miles to the knoll just beyond her fence.

So quiet and yet somewhere in her head, she heard a slight rumbling sound. She reached into her pocket and touched the key she had found in the dusty attic. As her fingers touched the key, the sound grew louder. Glancing once more at the scene outside, she turned and putting the key back in her pocket she made her way up the front stairs.

CHAPTER 27

Bridgitt sat at the kitchen table with her second cup of coffee. She found she was spending a lot of time on her own lately. With Jim's new job, he had very little time to spend with her. When he was home, he was strangely quiet and not willing to talk about his work or the time he spent in the village. They had always been close and able to talk about their respective days until just lately. It seemed that he was spending more and more time in the village in the evenings. Their house didn't seem important to him any longer. When they first arrived, he was always there to help with the painting or hanging pictures. It had been fun for both of them. Lately, she had the feeling the house was more hers and Jim had no part in it.

A sudden breeze blew the curtains at the window giving Bridgitt a sudden whiff of the wild roses that grew up the side of the porch. She loved those roses. That was the reason she had bought the wallpaper for the front hall. Jim had thought it was too much pattern and tried to talk her into taking it back for something plain. She had held out however but had never found the time to put it up.

She looked down into her coffee cup and realized it was empty. Going to the sink, she rinsed it and put it in the rack to dry. It would be hours before Jim got home, she thought. She would surprise him when he got home. Pulling the bag of wallpaper from the downstairs closet, she headed up the hall feeling much better than she had all day.

She cut the string holding the rolls together and let them fall to the floor. One by one they started to unroll across the floor. Bridgitt let the first one roll through her fingers. She laid it against the wall and sighed with pleasure as the roses seemed to twine upwards to the ceiling. One by one she guided the rolls across the floor to their spot on the walls. Soon she was surrounded by beautiful flowers. She curled up in the corner by the stairs and inhaled the wonderful perfume as the flowers made their home forever.

CHAPTER 28

Karen suddenly felt very tired. The upset of Joe's death, and the visit from the sheriff laid heavy on her mind. She couldn't imagine what the sheriff thought she would know about the local realtor. She had only met Shelby once when she first arrived and wasn't terribly impressed with her. She certainly wouldn't be starting up a chummy friendship with her now or in the near future. She had planned on doing a bit of work around the house, but she was so tired she decided to forgo it until another day. She wandered up the stairs with the intention of a short nap before dinner. As she started down the hallway, the door to the attic caught her attention. She was sure it was closed when she came down this morning and as far as she knew there had been no one up the stairs since. It would be just like that real estate woman to come snooping around when she was out as she hadn't locked the door when she left.

She eased the door open calling up the stairs. All was quiet; however, a look around might be a good idea since the door was open. She made her way up the dusty stairs and reached for the chain on the single light bulb. Even with the light on, there were dark shadows in the corners. Spooky, she thought as chills ran down her arms. Not a place to stay.

As she reached up to pull the light chain again, she noticed that the old trunk seemed to have shifted slightly. Hesitantly, she walked to the corner. Yes, it had been moved and the old lock that had appeared to be rusted shut hung loosely by the hinges. Slowly, she took hold of the hinge and began to open the lid. A sudden gust of wind pulled it from her hand, opening the trunk wide. Karen peered in the trunk. It seemed to be completely empty, but on looking closer, she noticed in the bottom of the trunk a small black journal.

Reaching down, Karen picked it up and turning it over in her hands was able to make out a name on the front cover. The journal was very old and the letters had faded over the years, but with a bit of dusting, she was able to make out the name, Bridgitt. Bridgitt, there was something familiar about that name. She opened the journal and started reading the first page. It was hard to make out the words in the poor lighting of the attic. She would take the journal down to her room where she would be able to read it more clearly.

Turning towards the door on the far wall, Karen reached into her pocket for the key. It was dark on this side of the room, and she wished she had taken time to find her flashlight. She was not even sure she would be able to see the keyhole in this light. Taking the key from her pocket, she felt around the door for a keyhole. Surprisingly, she found it at once and slipped the key in and turned. Slowly, the door opened, and Karen was surprised to see in spite of the darkness of the rest of the attic, this room was in full light. There were no cobwebs in sight, and the floor looked newly polished. Pushing the door wide, Karen was surprised to find the room furnished as well as clean.

A long table was set with a formal setting, and all decorations had been tended with great detail. The table was set with ebony black dishes accented by a beautiful pink cloth. The centerpiece was made up of black and pink, and the candles in the tapers on the table as well as all the candles in the room were black. There were 13 stately chairs set about the table with a black ribbon tied to its back.

As beautiful as it appeared, Karen suddenly felt a chill down her spine, and she backed slowly towards the door. She quietly slipped out, closing the door behind her. She stood for a moment with her back against the door. Why would someone set up such a room obviously to entertain when there was a perfectly beautiful dining room on the main floor?

She felt a sudden burning sensation in her hand and realized it was from the key she had used in the door. She quickly dropped it at her feet and backed away. As it struck the floor, it burst into fames and was gone. In terror, Karen backed out of the room and slammed the door. Light shone around the door edges and from the keyhole. She turned and hurried to the staircase.

Clutching the journal to her she started down the stairs. Karen's thoughts were so engrossed in the journal that she didn't notice the trunk lid slide slowly back into place and the hinges reattached themselves. Also, it did not occur to her that there was no way a breeze could get into the attic let alone blow open the lid to a heavy trunk. The dust settled once again as she closed the door, and the old trunk slipped slowly back into place.

CHAPTER 29

Sheriff Hennessey entered the quiet of the library. From the doorway, he could see Berta the librarian busy stamping a pile of books in front of her. Berta had been the librarian when as a boy he was just able on tip toes to see the top of her desk. He remembered going every Saturday morning to story time when Berta would weave magic for all the local kids. He remembered listening starry eyed about dragons and fairies and witches. Mostly, he remembered about the witches.

As a young lad, he remembered the stories about the Warren house and the tales about the witch who had lived there. Berta glanced up as he approached the desk.

"Good morning sheriff," she said. "What brings you here this morning? We have a new delivery of detective stories just arrived and I know you are partial to them."

"Not today, thanks Berta'" he replied. "Today, I need to look at some of the old newspapers you have on file. Something back in the eighteen hundreds."

"Then you need to go to our archives," she said, taking her ring of keys from the desk drawer. "Come along with me, and I'll show you where that period is. It's so much better now that everything has been put on film. No rummaging through boxes and boxes to find what you want, and the paper was getting so fragile I almost didn't want anyone to disturb them. Now I know everything is safe and people can read to their heart's content. Do you have any idea what year you are looking for?"

"Yes," the sheriff replied. "The year there was so much fuss up at the old Warren place. I remember the stories my grandfather used to tell me as a boy. My grandmother used to raise ned with him for trying to scare me."

"That's an old expression I haven't heard for some time," she said. "It was a favourite of my grandmother's." She opened the door to a room at the back of the library. "Here we are," she said. "I don't suppose I have to show you how things work do I?"

"No, I can take it from here thanks, Berta."

As the sheriff took a seat in front of one of the monitors, he heard Berta close the door quietly behind her. He thought what a quiet life Berta lived here every day and wondered if when she went home, if she stood inside her front door and doing a happy jig just screamed her head off. He smiled at the picture that would make with a woman easily in her late seventies.

Scrolling down through the news, he stopped on occasion coming across a clipping of interest that he had forgotten about over the years. There was the announcement about Wayne James triplets, brothers for their twin girls. The twins were only one year at the time and caused quite a bit of gossip around town for a while. It was wondered how poor May would be able to handle all those babies on her own as Wayne was not known to be very ambitious.

Thinking about them, the Sheriff nearly missed the year he was looking for. There it was. It was the summer of 1838. It had been a hot summer and when this happens it seems like the blood also runs hot leading to more than average crime. Jim and Bridgitt O'Hara had just moved into the village. Jim had been transferred from another branch of the lumber company taking over a supervisory position. They were a young couple newly married and had been given a house that belonged to the company as part of Jim's wages. The house was transferred into their name, and they settled in.

Jim had been a likable sort and seemed to ft into the pattern. His wife Bridgitt on the other hand spent most of her time at the house and so became a target of the local ladies' gossip. It was said, quoted by the ladies, that she was strange and that strange things were happening at the house. Rumors had it that at night some of the ladies had seen strange lights coming from the house and that one or two had seen strange purchases from the grocery store. It helped that the wife of the grocer could add her bit of news to this. The outcome had been a group of villagers had gone to the house one night to confront her. On arriving, they had found no one in the house although they had seen the lights go out as they were coming up the lane. Several of the men had searched the house, but there was no sign of her. It was the opinion of the villagers that what they had feared was that she was a witch and had been able to escape by some magic power she possessed. Bridgitt was never found and soon after the incident Jim transferred out of the area.

Sheriff Hennesey scrolled down further, but there was nothing further on the incident. It had been erased from the village memory. He did remember hearing though that not all of the people in the village approved of the actions that night and not all thought that Bridgitt was a witch.

It was said that Bridgitt had a brother somewhere and had come to claim the house and tried to find her whereabouts. In the back of his mind, he thought he remembered the brother's name, and there was something familiar about it. Maybe at some time it would come to him. Pushing back his chair, he turned off the machine and left the room. Thanking Berta for her time, he left the library and headed back to his office. He knew there would be telephone calls and messages on his desk, and he would be in for a busy day. Deciding to set this on the back burner for now until he had more time, he made his way up the main street to another day in the life of his village.

CHAPTER 30

Karen made her way down the stairs and into the front parlor. She took the journal and settled in one of the big chairs. Opening the book, she started reading the delicate handwritten pages. It was our first day in our new home, she read. It doesn't seem possible that we are so lucky. Everything here belongs to us. The house is a gift from the company where Jim works as part of his promotion. We are very excited about decorating the way we want it and tomorrow I will go into the village and buy paint and wallpaper so we can start.

Monday. Today I went shopping. I found wallpaper and new curtains for the kitchen with tablecloth and towels to match. Jim wanted blue and I wanted yellow, so we now have a kitchen of blue and yellow. I picked out enough wallpaper to do the bedroom and the front hall. It has a rose pattern the same color as the roses climbing up the back porch. Jim thinks it's too much pattern for the front hall and wants to take it back. I think I will put it in the front closet for a few days until Jim gets used to the pattern in the bedroom.

Friday. It's been three weeks now, and I just finished papering the front hall. It is the first thing you see when you come in the front door. I know when Jim sees it, he will love it as much as I do. Everyone in the village has been so friendly. It is nice to go shopping and have everyone say hello. I bought candles today for the dining room. When I finish everything, I would like to have a dinner party with some of the people from Jim's work. I think that pink and black candles will finish off the table nicely. I will have to check with Jim to see who we should ask.

Day after Party. I spent the day by myself crying. I had worked so hard for that dinner party, and then everything just fell apart. We started with drinks in the parlor and everyone seemed friendly until we went in for dinner. It was as if they were a different group of people. I had waited all day to show off my table. Everything was in pink and black.

I had found a set of black dishes in the attic and even black candles. They were beautiful with my pink cloth and napkins so I had placed the candles all through the room. Also, there was an intricate black centerpiece. The ladies were the first to reach the dining room, and I heard them gasp as they backed off. Turning to their husbands, they asked for their wraps.

Before I could ask why, they turned and left the house. So, the dinner I had taken so much time preparing was left in the kitchen to grow cold. Jim promised he would find out what had happened, and I cried myself to sleep in his arms.

Sunday. It has been eight weeks since the dreadful night of my dinner. I haven't been to the village as I don't want to meet the women I thought were friends. Jim was unable to get answers as to why everyone left. I suspect he knows something, but just isn't going to tell me. I put the black dishes back in the attic and packed a box with my cloth, napkins and the candles and put them away too. I may never go to the village again.

Thursday. Tomorrow is Halloween, and I decided to decorate. The garden is full of pumpkins so I can make jack-o-lanterns and cut witches out of black paper to pin on the curtains. It will give me something to do with my time as Jim spends most of his evenings in the village now. There is a fresh bushel basket of apples from the orchard to be given out to the local children if they come. Also, I could use the black candles to set out in the windows and through the house. The house looks just like a haunted house. Just what I wanted. The children will love it. When they see the popcorn balls I made to look like black cats swinging on a rope they will be so excited.

There was just a single entry on the next page. It is the day after Halloween, and no one came.

CHAPTER 31

Karen slowly closed the book. Why, they thought Bridgitt was a witch, because she decorated her house for Halloween? No, there had to be more to it than that. Bridgitt must have done something else for the town to turn against her. She was just about to continue reading again when she heard a car pull up in the front drive. Setting the book aside, she made her way to the front door. Pulling aside the curtain, she saw the sheriff just getting out of his car. Now what she thought? Soon she was going to make up a story just to get him off her back. It seemed like the truth wasn't working very well.

"Hello again, Sheriff," she said just opening the door enough to see out.

"Hello Karen. I was just driving by and happened to think of something I forgot to ask. Did you know that this house was originally owned by your great grandmother and grandfather? I believe it was on your mother's side which is why the name wasn't familiar to anyone.

"No, I didn't," Karen said. "I wasn't even aware the house existed until my father passed away, and then it came up in the will. I thought it must have been something my Dad bought as an investment and then never did anything about it. How did you find out it was a relative of mine when the family lawyer didn't know?"

"Just by chance actually. I was at the village library looking up an old news clipping when I came upon a news item that involved your house. Since it had never been sold, I checked to see who the property was registered to and your father's name came up as the last owner. It seems he inherited it as the last living relative, so when he passed away, it was transferred to you. The house has never had a very good reputation. As a matter of fact, over the years it was known as the local haunted house. Seems there was some witchcraft involved back in the eighteen hundreds. Witchcraft was a popular notion back then and it didn't take much for new people coming into the area to be branded as such. Anyway, I just thought I would pass that on to you in case some of the local gossip clubs decided to start up the story again. Also, I wanted you to know that I can be here in a matter of minutes if you need me."

"Thank you, Sheriff, but I think in this century I am safe from being branded a witch just because of some foolish story in the eighteenth century. I hope we have progressed further than that."

"Just the same," the sheriff said, "if you need me, I'll be there." Sheriff Hennesey sat for a moment in his car before he pulled out his phone and dialed a number. When a voice answered he said, "tell them it's starting again, and they will know what to do."

Karen watched as the sheriff pulled out of the drive. What a funny man, she thought. Did he really think that the village might view her as a descendant of a witch? She was still smiling when she took her seat once more and opened Bridgitt's journal.

CHAPTER 32

Edna Thornton dropped her window curtain just as the sheriff's car pulled away. All this time and nothing and now it was starting again. She wondered if she were to warn Karen she should leave before it was too late. That might be the only way to save her. Edna hadn't been out of her house for years. It had been her job as a watcher to keep tabs on the house next door. Between herself and Joe they had been put in charge to make sure the house was not disturbed. It had been a long tiresome job as the various village children over the years had been tempted to enter the house to see if it was haunted. No one was to enter the house and for many years no one did until now.

Who was to know that a descendent would actually come to live there? It had been passed down quietly through the family without a problem until now. The last owner died and left it to his daughter who decided she wanted to see what she had inherited. Shelby was supposed to set it up right away for a sale to one of the locals who would in turn keep it from being lived in. Where was that girl anyway? It wasn't like her to stay away so long. Even on a holiday Edna knew where her niece was until this time. She would certainly give her a piece of her mind when she got back from wherever she was. It looked like she would have to go to

Karen herself. She just couldn't leave her over there not knowing the danger she was in.

Pushing herself away from the window, she reached for her cane. It might be nice to talk to someone besides Shelby for a change. Going to the closet, she pulled her coat from the rack and wound a silk scarf around her neck. She tucked the small wisps of white hair back behind her ears and checked her appearance in the small mirror on the back of the door.

Just as she was turning away, she thought she saw movement in the far corner of the room. She hadn't noticed how dark it had become. Funny it wasn't that late in the day. There must be a storm brewing. As she reached for the door handle, she felt the silk scarf tightening around her neck. Reaching up she tried to loosen it. There didn't seem to be a reason for it to tighten. She set her cane against the wall and pulled at the scarf with both hands. Still the scarf tightened until she could no longer breathe. She tried calling out, but the scarf became tighter and she slowly sank to her knees by the door. The last thing she remembered before darkness was the sound of a woman's laughter, and the sharp pain tightening in her chest.

CHAPTER 33

Karen started reading where she left off. It was a bit hard to follow as Bridgitt never actually dated the pages just days and sometimes not even that.

Monday. I never go to the village anymore, the children taunt me, they call me a witch, and I see women talking behind their hands. Funny, these same women were the ones who welcomed me when I came to the village. It doesn't matter as I have plenty to do here in the house. I won't let a group of narrow-minded old women spoil things for Jim and I. Jim will not be as busy at night soon and when he can stay home more the house will be all done and ready for him. Then we can sit out on the terrace, smell the roses and watch the fireflies or fairies as mother called them.

Thursday. I found more things in the attic today. Some of them my brother Sam would like. Funny, I don't think about Sam too much anymore. He was the black sheep of the family, and after he married and moved away, we lost track of him. These old pictures of family groups would interest him. He was always delving into the family history. Some of them look familiar. I can't see how that would be as I have never been in this part of the country before. They do say everyone has a double. Maybe they resemble someone I know back home. Whoever lived here must have liked the color black as all the clothes in the old trunk were black. I found two other books and an old journal that I will take downstairs and read when I have a few moments.

Tuesday. I read some of the journal today. I felt sorry for the girl who had written it. I know by the handwriting it must have been a girl as most men do not have such fine penmanship. I think she must have spent many days alone. She mentions a husband who was away a lot leaving her on her own. I know what that is like as Jim still spends most of his nights with the men in the village, and when he is home, he is very distant. I wonder where the Jim I married is? Until we came here, he laughed all the time and teased me until I cried. I would give anything to have that old Jim back. Well, it's time to start supper just in case Jim comes home tonight.

Karen set the journal aside once more. She couldn't seem to put the story together. She didn't know how she knew that there would be no end to this story. The journal would never be finished. She hadn't noticed how dark the room had become. It would be good to light some candles in here. Candles always gave a nice soft feel to a room. She opened the cabinet door where she had stored her extra candles. Fixing them into holders, she placed them around the room. As she started towards the door, she turned once to look back. Yes, they did look nice, and the black candles were just the right color for the room. Quietly, she closed the door and headed for the kitchen.

CHAPTER 34

Karen stood at the kitchen window looking out at the house next door. Everything was quiet, there were no lights burning in what Karen knew was the old lady's library. The lights always seemed more ethereal than normal lighting. Like the light of a thousand fireflies flashing all at one time. As a small child, her mother told her they were fairy lights and many nights Karen had watched from her window hoping to catch a glimpse of one of the tiny creatures. Now once again as if swept back into the past, she watched in vain. She shook herself from her thoughts.

Dan would be coming soon and she had yet to start dinner. Funny when she had come to the village it was to sell the house her father had left her in his will. She had taken a leave of absence just to tie up loose ends on the sale. However, once she arrived, she felt a deep pull by the house to keep her here. Then she had met Dan and knew she could not just leave and go back to the life she had led before. It had been an instant reaction with Dan. One she wanted to pursue until she knew the end results.

They had both wanted more time together, so she had called her office and told them she would be staying longer than the initial time she had allotted. Fortunately, they agreed and she had settled into her house to see where her life would go from here.

Dan, warm feelings went through her every time she thought of him. She thought about living with him here in her house.

She was suddenly broken from her reverie by a low rumbling sound. It seemed to be coming from her side yard. Possibly from the old lady's house. She lifted the kitchen curtains to see. The sound was there alright, but she couldn't see what was causing it. Nothing was visible. Dropping the curtain, she busied herself with the vegetables in the sink. The rumble seemed much louder. A familiar sound she thought, almost like a pack of horses at the race track.

Once more, she pulled back the curtains to look out. Dropping them in fright, she tried to register in her mind what she had just seen. The noise was deafening. With trembling fingers, Karen once more pulled the curtains aside. The old lady's house was gone. There was nothing there but a vast field with a long winding road cutting through it. It was through this field that the sound came. She strained to see if there was anything that would cause it. Then she saw them.

Over the horizon, a faint light was making its way up the road. It bounced from earth to sky as it made its way along. Not unlike fairy lights, she thought. It appeared to be coming toward her, and as it did, sudden fear took her. They are coming for me again, she thought. Where was Jim? She was so afraid there alone without him. If he would only come home, she knew everything would be alright. She turned off the kitchen light and made her way into the front hall. If she turned off all the lights and was very quiet, they would think there was no one there. She reached over and touched the switch in the hall, and everything went dark. Now she had only to wait.

Suddenly, there was a loud roar and crashing on the front steps. Karen backed away up the staircase. She heard voices at the front steps.

"She's in there," a male voice said. "I saw the lights go out just as we turned on the lane."

"Break down the door," another voice called. "We will have that witch before we leave here."

Karen froze, they had called her a witch. Were these the people she had come to know in the past few weeks? She had thought they were becoming her friends. What was she going to do? She could hear the cracking of wood as the front door split. She knew more fear than she had ever known in her life. She would have to hide, but where?

Suddenly, there was a cool breeze in the staircase, and she was aware of the fragrance of lilacs. "Touch the walls," a voice said. "Touch the walls Karen, and you will be safe with me. Just touch the walls." The noise at the door grew louder. It would break soon, and they would be upon her. She had no choice. Looking at the roses and lilacs intertwined, she reached forward and touched the wall. Then she was gone.

CHAPTER 35

Dan had been knocking on the door for some time before he realized there could be something wrong. He knew Karen was in there because he had seen the lights go out as he came up the lane to the house. It had suddenly become very dark with only his headlights to show him the way. Looking up, he thought he saw a shadow in the bedroom window. He knocked again this time calling Karen's name. He suddenly felt panic as there was no response. Dan knew he had to get into the house.

With all the force he could manage, he put his shoulder to the door until he heard the wood split beneath it. Reaching in, he turned the knob and entered the hall. As he made his way through the house calling her name, a cold hand of fear took hold of him. She had to be here somewhere, she couldn't just disappear into the walls. Making his way back to the hallway, he turned on the light. It seemed colder here than in the rest of the house, and he was sure he could smell lilacs.

He glanced up the staircase. There was something different about it. On a closer look, he found that the paper not only had roses but intertwined through the bright pink roses were small bunches of lilacs.

He stepped forward for a better look and leaning forward, he felt a soft touch on his shoulder. Quickly, he pulled back. Something told him to leave and leave now. When he reached the front door, he touched the light switch plunging everything into darkness. As an afterthought, he pulled together the damaged front door. He would wait until it was light to fix the door.

As he went down the steps, he did not hear the voice behind calling, "Don't leave Dan. I am here." Also had he looked up again, he would have seen two shadows in the upstairs window looking down at him. Starting the engine, he made his way up the drive and away from the house. In the house next door, the lace curtains on the window dropped slowly into place and silence settled over the countryside once more.

EPILOGUE

The dark grey sedan made its way slowly up the lane. Rachael peered out between the trees for the first vision of her new home. It had been a surprise when she received the call from her lawyer notifying her of her good fortune. Apparently, it was an old family home in a small village near Boston. It had been empty for five years since the disappearance of Karen Warren, a cousin of Rachael's. Since she was the next living relative, and no other claim had been entered against it the house was now hers.

She had only met Karen as a small child when her parents had come to visit, bringing her with them. They had both been the same age at the time. Karen's parents never returned and Rachael's parents had never gone to visit them so this had been her only connection with Karen. Now here she was inheriting Karen's house.

The lane began to widen as she neared the house, and Rachael lowered her window for a better view. There it was tall and stately in the sunshine. She was so excited she could hardly wait for the cab to stop. The driver pulled over to the wide steps leading up to the front veranda, and Rachael jumped from the car. Clapping her hands with excitement, she barely took time to pay the driver and tell him to just leave her bags on the steps.

It was so beautiful, she thought and hers. Making her way around the side of the house she noticed that there was another house very close to hers and that someone was working on the hedge. This must be the gardener the lawyer had told her about. Apparently, he had looked after the house for many years and had made sure everything was ready for her arrival. She walked toward him, her hand out in greeting.

The old gardener looked up as she approached and wiping his hands on his worn overalls smiled as he said, "Good morning Miss, I am Joe your gardener. It is so nice to have someone coming to live here once more." Rachael shook hands and noticed at the window next door a slight flutter of curtains and a tiny tinkle of laughter. Rachael looked around the gardens. Such beautiful roses and lilac trees. She sighed with happiness. She was home.

www.ingramcontent.com/pod-product-compliance
Lightning Source LLC
LaVergne TN
LVHW091933070526
838200LV00068B/960